THE
COLOR
OF PIECES

OVERCOMING PAIN, RECLAIMING POWER, AND
EMBRACING NEW BEGINNINGS

BY MICHELLE E. RHONEY

ISBN: 979-8-9928797-1-1 (Paperback)

ISBN: 979-8-9928797-0-4 (Hardcover)

ISBN: 979-8-9928797-2-8 (eBook)

Book design by Dara Publishing LLC

Place of Publication: Essex, Maryland, 21221

Library of Congress: 2025906854

Printed in the United States of America.

Disclaimer: This is a work of autobiographical fiction. While inspired by true events, names, characters, places, and incidents have been altered, fictionalized, or adapted to serve the narrative. Any resemblance to actual persons, living or deceased, or real-life events is purely coincidental or used fictitiously. The author has made every effort to respect privacy and ensure that any real-life experiences have been presented with integrity and discretion. The opinions expressed are those of the author and do not reflect any official stance of organizations, institutions, or individuals mentioned.

DEDICATION

Dear 17-Year-Old Me,

I know you feel like you have to have it all figured out right now. You're standing at the edge of adulthood, eager to prove yourself, afraid to fail, and wondering if you are enough. Let me tell you this: you are. You always have been, and you always will be.

Confidence isn't about being perfect. It isn't about fitting in or being who others expect you to be. Confidence is about knowing your worth, even when the world tries to make you doubt it. It's about walking into a room and not needing validation because you already know who you are. So, stop shrinking yourself to make others comfortable. Speak up. Take up space. Be bold enough to trust your voice.

When it comes to love, please remember this: real love will never require you to lose yourself. You will meet people who will try to define love on their terms, who will make you think you have to change to be worthy of it. But love is not about sacrifice at the cost of your identity. The right kind of love will celebrate you, not diminish you. Love yourself first—so deeply that you never settle for less than you deserve.

Take pride in who you are, where you come from, and in the dreams that seem too big right now. One day, you will look back and realize that the things you were most insecure about were actually your greatest strengths. Stand tall in your truth. Own your journey. You do not have to apologize for being who you were meant to be.

And above all, respect yourself. Set boundaries without guilt. Say no without explaining yourself. Surround yourself with people who pour into you, not just those who take. Respect your mind, your heart, and your body enough to protect them from those who do not see your value.

Life will challenge you. It will break you in ways you never expected. But it will also rebuild you, shape you, and turn you into the woman you are destined to become. So, hold your head high. Trust the journey. And never forget—there is nothing more powerful than a girl who believes in herself.

With love and wisdom,
Me

TABLE OF CONTENTS

"You may not control all the events that happen to you, but you can decide not to be reduced by them."

Maya Angelou

PREFACE

I know what it feels like to lose myself in love, to break, to question my worth, and to wonder if I will ever feel whole again. I wrote this book for the woman still picking up the pieces, for the one who feels unseen, unheard, and uncertain about her next step.

This book is a reflection of resilience, a testament to healing, and a reminder that no matter how shattered life may feel, we are never beyond repair. I wanted to create something that speaks to the hearts of women learning to embrace their past without being defined by it. I wrote it to remind them that pain does not get the final say—strength, love, and self-discovery do.

Most of all, I wrote this book because I have lived this journey. I know firsthand that healing is not linear. Some days, it means moving forward with confidence; other days, it means revisiting wounds I thought had healed. But through it all, I have learned that there is hope. There is growth. And there is power in choosing yourself, again and again.

This book is my love letter to every woman who has ever felt broken, reminding her that she is already whole.

INTRODUCTION

*W*hat happens when the life you thought you had carefully built begins to crumble, piece by piece? When love, trust, and security slip through your fingers like sand, leaving you to question everything you once believed? How do you gather the fragments of a shattered past and rebuild a life that feels whole again?

This book is about that journey.

At its core, *The Color of Pieces* is a story of transformation, resilience, and the power of self-worth. It explores what it means to lose yourself—and what it takes to find your way back. Through the lens of Lola, a woman who has loved deeply, lost painfully, and fought to reclaim her voice, it delves into the complexities of healing, the courage to let go, and the beauty of rediscovering your power.

Although this is a work of fiction, it's rooted in autobiography— so the emotions, struggles, and victories within these pages are deeply personal. The details may be fictionalized, but the pain is real. The heartbreak is real. The lessons are real. I've lived them— and if you are holding this book, perhaps you have, too.

WHY THIS STORY? WHY NOW?

For a long time, I believed healing meant forgetting—that to move forward, I had to erase the past. But healing isn't about erasure. It's about understanding, accepting, and honoring the experiences that shaped you. It's about looking at the broken pieces of your past not with regret but with gratitude for the wisdom they've given you.

I wrote this book because I know what it's like to question your worth, to wonder if you're enough after loss, betrayal, and disappointment. I know how it feels to be a stranger in your own life, trapped in a cycle of pain and self-doubt. But I also know the power of choosing yourself—of standing in the mirror, scars and all, and saying, "I am worthy."

Lola's story reflects that truth.

THE JOURNEY THROUGH THE PIECES

Throughout this book, you'll walk with Lola as she navigates love, heartbreak, grief, and self-discovery. You'll see her lose herself in relationships that drained her, mourn a love taken too soon, and wrestle with the uncertainty of who she is beyond the roles she's played. You'll feel her pain—but you'll also witness her rise, piece by piece, choice by choice, moment by moment.

This book isn't just about pain; it's about redemption. It's about the women who surround us, lift us, and remind us who we are. It's about the power of friendship, faith, and self-love. It's about daring to believe that even after life has broken you, you can still build something beautiful, meaningful, and true.

FOR THE READER HOLDING THIS BOOK

This book is for you if you've ever lost yourself in love, questioned your worth, or struggled to move forward after heartbreak. It is for the woman who is learning to embrace her past without letting it define her. It is for those who have felt unseen, unheard, and unsure of their next step.

If you're still piecing your life back together, know this: you are not alone. You are not broken beyond repair. The pieces of your story—no matter how painful, messy, or complicated—are part of something greater. They're shaping you into the woman you're meant to become.

Healing isn't a straight path. It's a journey of setbacks, realizations, and breakthroughs. Some days, you'll feel like you've moved forward. On other days, you may face the same wounds you thought had healed. That's okay. Give yourself grace. Give yourself time. But never stop choosing yourself.

The Power of Telling Our Stories

Women have been taught for generations to suffer in silence—to carry our wounds in secret, to shrink ourselves so others feel comfortable. But what happens when we refuse to stay silent? When we claim our truth and say, "This is my story, and I will no longer be ashamed of it?"

The Color of Pieces is an act of defiance against that silence. It's a declaration that our pain matters, our voices matter, and healing is possible. This book is a reminder that sharing our stories doesn't make us weak—it makes us powerful.

A FINAL INVITATION

The Color of Pieces is not just my story—it is ours. It is for every woman who has stood before a mirror and struggled to recognize the reflection staring back at her. It is for anyone who has felt like they were drowning in their past, uncertain if they'd ever feel whole again.

I invite you to step into this story with an open heart. Let Lola's journey remind you of your own strength. Let her pain remind you of your own resilience. Let her healing be a mirror of what is possible for you.

You are not merely surviving—you are becoming. You are worthy of joy, love, and purpose. Even when you feel like you're falling apart, trust that you are being shaped into something greater.

There is life beyond pain. Hope beyond heartbreak. Beauty in the pieces.

As you turn the pages, I hope you find not just Lola's story but your own.

Walk with me now, page by page—one piece at a time.

Chapter 1

BECOMING WHOLE

> *"I wasn't just building something—
> I was healing."*

The conference was a milestone—but only the beginning of my journey. The energy in the room that day was electric: women laughing, crying, and sharing stories long buried in their hearts. It was proof that our shared experiences held power, and I was determined to harness that power to create lasting change.

In the months that followed, I poured my heart and soul into building what I now call *The Color of Pretty Foundation*. It had grown beyond colorism—it was about self-worth, confidence, and creating spaces where women felt seen and celebrated. I envisioned a safe haven, a place where women and young girls could unlearn the harmful messages they'd internalized and step into their full potential.

I started small, hosting intimate workshops in community centers, schools, and churches. Each session reaffirmed why I began this mission. Women from all walks of life came forward, sharing how society's expectations and prejudices had shaped their self-image. I listened, held hands, wiped tears, and reminded them of their worth.

One story stayed with me. A young woman named Aisha, barely 20, stood up during a session. Her voice trembled as she described growing up in a family that favored her lighter-skinned siblings, leaving her feeling invisible.

"I've always felt like I had to overcompensate for not being 'enough'—not pretty enough, not smart enough, *just not enough*," she said through tears.

I walked over, pulled her into a tight hug, and whispered, "You are more than enough. Don't let anyone tell you otherwise."

As I stepped away, I saw my younger self in her. The pain in her eyes mirrored the battles I'd fought within myself for years. It deepened my commitment to ensuring The Color of Pretty wasn't just a one-time event—it was a movement.

The foundation expanded rapidly. We launched mentorship programs, partnered with mental health professionals, and introduced initiatives like *Letters to My Younger Self*, where women across the country wrote messages of encouragement and self-love to their past selves. The campaign went viral, and soon, *The Color of Pretty* was being talked about in spaces I had only dreamed of reaching.

I wasn't just building an organization—I was healing. With every story shared, every breakthrough witnessed, and every life impacted, I reclaimed pieces of myself that had once been shattered.

This was bigger than me now. This was a revolution.

With each passing month, *The Color of Pretty* grew beyond anything I had imagined. What began as a single conference had evolved into a full-fledged movement—one that was reshaping how women saw themselves, their beauty, and their worth. I found myself speaking on panels, interviewed for podcasts, and featured in articles highlighting the foundation's impact.

But the recognition wasn't what mattered most—it was the stories.

One evening, as I sifted through emails, I came across a message from a woman named Simone:

"Lola, I don't know if you'll ever read this, but I just wanted to say thank you. For years, I struggled with self-hate because of my dark skin. I used to pray to be lighter, to be 'prettier.' But after attending one of your workshops, something in me shifted. I see myself differently now. I don't cringe when I look in the mirror—I smile. And that's because of you."

Tears welled up in my eyes. This was why I did it.

The foundation kept expanding in ways I never expected. We launched *Confidence Camp*, a summer program for teenage girls focused on self-esteem, leadership, and resilience. We partnered with beauty brands that aligned with our mission, advocating for representation in campaigns and product lines. And as our influence grew, so did the community of women committed to breaking generational cycles of self-doubt.

THE EXPANSION

As *The Color of Pretty* grew, so did I. I wasn't just creating a movement—I was evolving within it. Every conference, every workshop, and every heartfelt conversation reminded me that my pain had purpose. That my journey, with all its twists and turns, wasn't just mine to carry—it was meant to be shared, to light the way for others still struggling to see their own worth.

I poured myself into expanding the foundation's reach, collaborating with therapists, scholars, and activists to build programs that addressed self-esteem, mental health, and mentorship for young girls and women. We led workshops on body positivity, hosted panel discussions on the impact of colorism, and partnered with schools to implement self-love curricula.

One of our most powerful initiatives, *Letters to My Younger Self*, sparked a nationwide response. As thousands of women shared their truths, I found myself deeply moved—not just by their stories but by what they stirred in me. Their words reopened quiet places in my own heart, urging me to face memories I had long tucked away. It became clear that I, too, had something to say to the girl I once was.

So, I wrote my own:

Dear Lola,

You are enough. Even when they tell you you're too much, too dark, too loud—remember, you are enough. Don't dim your light to make others comfortable. Don't shrink to fit into spaces that were never meant for you. You are beautiful, strong, and worthy of all the good things life has to offer. One day, you'll look back on this moment and realize it was all part of your journey to becoming the woman you were meant to be.

Keep going.
Love, Me.

The campaign went viral. Letters poured in from across the country—from mothers, daughters, grandmothers, and young girls who had long been waiting for permission to love themselves. Social media flooded with testimonies as women shared their letters, their tears, and their truths.

In that moment, I realized *The Color of Pretty* had become something far greater than I ever imagined. It was no longer just about colorism or societal beauty standards—it was about identity, self-worth, and breaking the generational cycles of insecurity that had weighed us down for too long.

We were rewriting our narratives. And for the first time, I wasn't just urging others to believe in their beauty—I truly believed in my own.

As the foundation continued to flourish, so did my sense of purpose. I was no longer just surviving—I was thriving. My days were filled with speaking engagements, mentorship sessions, and strategy meetings to expand *The Color of Pretty*. Every day, I watched women and girls break free from the limitations that once held them back. The work was exhausting, but it was exhilarating.

One evening, after wrapping up a mentorship session, I sat in my office reflecting on how far I'd come. Just a few years ago, I had been the one searching for answers, trying to quiet the voices of self-doubt. Now, I was the one offering guidance, helping others find their own voices. It was a full-circle moment, and I let myself feel it fully.

Then, my phone buzzed.

Audra: *Girl, have you eaten today?*

I smiled. My tribe never let me slip.

Me: *Barely. Does coffee count?*

Audra: *Absolutely not. We're pulling up in 30. Be ready.*

True to her word, Audra, Latonya, and Karen arrived at my doorstep, armed with takeout and an agenda. They knew I would go full speed ahead if left to my own devices, and they weren't having it.

"Look at you," Latonya teased as she handed me a plate. "Running a whole movement but can't even feed yourself."

"I was going to eat," I protested weakly, taking a bite.

Karen raised an eyebrow. "Sure, you were."

I laughed, grateful for these women who kept me grounded. They weren't just friends—they were my rock. Through heartbreak, reinvention, and success, they had stood by me, reminding me of who I was when I'd forgotten.

As we ate, we talked about everything—life, love, new opportunities. I shared my excitement about the second annual *Color of Pretty* conference, which was shaping up to be bigger than ever.

"You know what's crazy?" I said, setting down my fork. "I never imagined this. Not like this."

Audra nodded. "That's the beauty of stepping into your purpose. You don't always see the full picture—you just have to trust the process."

And I had. I trusted it, even when it scared me. Even when I doubted whether I was enough.

As the night wound down, I realized something: I had spent so much of my life searching—for validation, for love, for something to make me feel whole. But now, in this moment, surrounded by my friends and fulfilled by my purpose, I finally felt it.

Peace.

And for the first time in a long time, I wasn't chasing happiness—I was living it.

Chapter 2

THE PERSONAL SHIFT

"A shift within is the first step toward creating the life you've always wanted."

---

*A*mid the whirlwind of building my foundation, I found myself in a place I hadn't expected: peace. Not the fleeting kind that rises and falls with circumstances, but a deep, unshakable peace—the kind that settles into your bones when you stop proving, stop performing, and simply allow yourself to be. For the first time in years, I wasn't chasing approval or trying to fit a mold that was never meant for me. I was discovering who Lola truly was—and to my surprise, I liked her.

It showed in how I moved, how I spoke, even how I carried myself. I no longer shrank to make others comfortable. I took up space—unapologetically. And if I had any doubts that something within me had shifted, Mikaela erased them one evening over dinner.

She had come home for a break from college, her energy filling the house and making it feel whole again. We sat at the table, just the two of us sharing a simple meal and catching up on life.

"Mom, you're glowing," she said, tilting her head as she studied me. It wasn't just an observation—it was a knowing.

I set my fork down, taken aback. "I guess I'm finally learning to love myself," I admitted, a slow smile spreading across my face.

"About time," she teased, shaking her head with a smirk, though her eyes shimmered with something deeper—pride.

We had come so far. The wounds that once felt impossible to heal had become scars—evidence of our survival, our resilience. Therapy wasn't just a process for us; it was a *lifeline*. It gave us the tools to rebuild what I once believed was broken beyond repair.

We laughed more, talked more, and leaned on each other in ways we never had before. The walls built from years of unspoken hurt and misunderstanding were gone, replaced by something much stronger: understanding.

For the first time in a long time, I wasn't just surviving—I was *living*.

LOVE REDEFINED

What I hadn't anticipated on this journey of self-discovery was the possibility of finding love again. Enter Nathan. We met at a networking event for nonprofit leaders, and his kindness caught me off guard. He wasn't flashy or boastful—just genuine.

"I've read about your foundation. What you're doing is incredible," he said during our first conversation. "Thank you," I replied, somewhat guarded. But as we talked, I found myself opening up.

Nathan wasn't just interested in my accomplishments— he wanted to know me. He listened intently, asked thoughtful questions, and never made me feel like I had to shrink myself. It was unfamiliar territory, but I allowed myself to explore it step by step.

As we continued to cross paths at various events, Nathan's presence became a quiet, steady force in my life. He never pushed or rushed—he simply showed up. Whether it was a quick coffee before a panel discussion or a late-night conversation about life, purpose, and everything in between, he made space for me in a way that felt different.

One evening, after a particularly emotional mentorship session, I felt drained—physically and emotionally. As if sensing it, Nathan called.

"Hey, just checking in. How was your day?"

I sighed, leaning back on the couch. "Heavy. But good. The girls I mentor… they're so full of potential, but they don't always see it. I just want them to know they're enough, just as they are."

"You do that every day, Lola," he said, his voice gentle but steady. "You show up for them. You remind them. And I hope you remind yourself, too."

His words stayed with me long after we hung up.

Over time, the walls I had so carefully built began to lower. Love didn't erase the past—but it honored it and allowed me to move forward.

Nathan was patient—never making me feel like I had to rush my healing. He understood that my heart had endured loss, that trust wasn't easily given, and that my independence wasn't up for negotiation. Rather than trying to change me, he embraced every part of who I was.

The first time Mikaela met him, I watched closely, unsure how she'd respond. She had always been my protector, fiercely looking out for me.

"So, Nathan," she said over dinner, giving him her best *I'm-watching-you* look. "What's your deal?"

He chuckled, completely unfazed. "My deal is that I think your mom is an incredible woman, and I just want to get to know her."

Mikaela smirked and nodded. "Good answer."

It wasn't instant, but slowly, piece by piece, a new kind of love found its way into my life. Love that was patient. Love that was steady. Love that reminded me I was worthy—not just of giving, but of receiving.

For the first time in a long time, I allowed myself to believe that maybe—just maybe—love wasn't something I had lost. It was something I was redefining.

I sat across from Mikaela, watching as she toyed with her fork, her expression unreadable. I knew this conversation was coming. I'd seen the curiosity in her eyes the moment she met Nathan. Now we were at the kitchen table, the weight of unspoken questions thick in the air.

I took a breath, choosing my words carefully. "Mikaela, I know you probably have questions about Nathan, and I want to be honest with you. He's a friend—someone who's been supportive during this chapter of my life."

She raised an eyebrow, unconvinced. "A friend, huh?"

I nodded, folding my hands. "Yes. Right now, my focus is on my career, the foundation, my business—and most importantly, you. Everything I'm doing is to build something meaningful, something lasting. I'm not looking for anything serious. Nathan is just someone who listens. Someone I trust."

Mikaela studied me for a moment as if weighing my words. Then, she exhaled and leaned back in her chair. "I get it, Mom. I just want to make sure you're okay. You've been through so much, and I don't want anyone to come in and messing with your peace."

Her words warmed my heart. She had always been protective of me, more than I sometimes realized. I reached across the table, squeezing her hand. "I appreciate that, baby girl. And trust me, I'm being careful. But I also know that healing doesn't always look like what we expect. Sometimes, it means letting people in— even if it's just as friends."

She smirked. "Just a friend, huh?"

I laughed. "Yes, Mikaela. Just a friend."

And at that moment, I realized how much I had grown. I wasn't rushing into anything or seeking validation in another person. I was standing firmly in who I was, embracing the life I had built, and allowing myself the space to explore what the future held—on my own terms.

The truth is, I wasn't even physically attracted to Nathan. He's not my type in that way, and he knows that. But he's smart as a whip, and right now, I need his guidance and support more than anything else. He's been a mentor, a sounding board, and someone I can lean on when things get overwhelming. And he's okay with that."

When Nathan was in the restroom, Mikaela studied me, her sharp intuition scanning for cracks in my explanation. "So, no romantic feelings at all?"

I shook my head firmly. "Nope. And that's the beautiful part of it—there's no pressure, no expectations. Just a genuine friendship. He understands that my focus right now is on my career, my foundation, my business, and, most importantly, you. That's where my heart is. Nathan and I have an understanding, and I'm grateful for the role he plays in my life, but that's it."

And for the first time in my life, I meant it. There was something freeing about that—about having a man in my life who wasn't expecting anything from me, who wasn't waiting for me to fall in love with him. For the first time, I was standing firm in who I was, embracing my growth, my healing, and my journey—on my own terms.

FULL CIRCLE

A year after the first *Color of Pretty* conference, I found myself back on stage for the second annual event. The energy in the room was electric—women from all walks of life filled every seat, their eyes reflecting hope, curiosity, and a hunger for something more. The quiet hum of conversation and the anticipation in the air felt familiar yet entirely new.

I took a deep breath and stepped forward, gripping the microphone, letting the moment settle over me. I had stood here before, but this time was different. I wasn't just telling a story—I was living proof of what's possible.

"Good evening, beautiful souls," I began, my voice steady and warm. "Last year, I stood here sharing my story, unsure of what the future held. I poured out my heart, my fears, my truths, hoping someone would find strength in my vulnerability. Today, I stand before you not as the woman I was but as the woman I've become— someone who knows her worth, embraces her imperfections, and celebrates the beauty in herself and others."

I scanned the room, meeting faces that held countless untold stories—young girls clinging to every word, mothers nodding in quiet understanding, grandmothers smiling with the wisdom of lived experience. Their presence reminded me this journey was no longer just mine—it was ours.

Applause erupted, filling the space with a powerful force of unity and shared triumph. In that moment, I knew this was more than a conference. It was a movement. A revolution of self-love, healing, and rediscovering the power within.

As the cheers softened, I smiled and let the words that had become my mantra flow from my heart.

"Confidence looks good on you. Wear it boldly, unapologetically, and proudly. Because you are enough."

And as the standing ovation echoed around me, I knew I wasn't just creating an event; I was building a legacy.

Chapter 3

REDEFINING MY PATH

"Sometimes, you must lose yourself to find the strength to rebuild a better version of who you are."

I began dating again—cautiously but with optimism. After the heartache and hard lessons of past relationships, I was determined to do things differently. My standards were higher, my boundaries clearer, and my self-love unwavering. Every dinner, coffee date, and conversation became a chance to learn—not just about the person across from me but about myself.

Still, dating wasn't my only focus. My career was flourishing in ways I had never imagined. By day, I thrived in my full-time role as a Human Resources leader, navigating the complexities of people management, organizational strategy, and executive decision-making. My voice carried weight in rooms where critical business choices were made, and I was gaining recognition for blending people-first leadership with company goals.

Outside of work, my consulting business was growing rapidly. What began as a side project had become a full-fledged enterprise, drawing in larger projects, high-profile clients, and opportunities that pushed me to expand my skills. I was advising organizations on talent development, diversity and inclusion, and leadership training—areas I cared deeply about. Each successful engagement affirmed I was walking in my purpose.

Speaking engagements had become a cornerstone of my professional journey. I was invited to share insights at conferences, corporate summits, and leadership retreats, standing before rooms filled with ambitious professionals seeking guidance. Every time I stepped onto a stage, I felt an electric connection with the audience. I wasn't just giving speeches—I was igniting transformation and confidence in those who, like me, had once questioned their potential.

However, perhaps the most fulfilling part of my work was mentoring young women to find their footing in their industries. I saw pieces of my younger self in them—the ambition, the fear, the drive to prove themselves. I took that role seriously, offering advice, coaching through difficult decisions, and being the support I once wished I had. Watching them grow, celebrating their wins, and knowing I played a small part in their success filled me in a way no corporate title ever could.

Balancing it all was demanding, but I thrived on the challenge. The late nights, early mornings, and back-to-back meetings were exhausting at times, but I reminded myself—I had prayed for and worked for this. I wasn't just climbing the corporate ladder; I was building my own empire, one opportunity at a time. More importantly, I was living my purpose, making an impact, and stepping into the most empowered version of myself yet.

The *Color of Pretty* movement opened doors I hadn't even imagined. I became a consultant for organizations seeking to create inclusive environments and empower women in the workplace.

One day, while preparing for a meeting, an email stopped me in my tracks. A publishing house was interested in turning my story into a book. They had heard about my conferences and believed my journey could inspire an even wider audience. I was stunned.

"Me? Write a book?" I laughed aloud, disbelief in my voice, as I called my best friend to share the news.

"Of course, you should!" she said, her excitement contagious. "You've been writing this story your whole life—now it's just time to put it on paper."

So I did. Every night after work, I poured my heart into my laptop, revisiting memories that made me cry, laugh, and everything in between. Writing wasn't just about sharing my story—it became a healing process.

But life wasn't all work. Mikaela was thriving in college, and our relationship had grown stronger than ever. One evening, she called, her voice brimming with pride.

"Mom, guess what? I got into the leadership program I applied for!"

"That's amazing, Mikaela!" I said, my heart swelling with pride. "I'm so proud of you."

"And guess what else?" she added with a giggle. "They want me to speak at the end-of-year ceremony. Looks like I'm following in your footsteps."

Hearing her say that was the ultimate validation. I wasn't just rebuilding my life—I was helping build hers, too.

One weekend, Mikaela came home for a visit, and we decided to clean out the garage. Amid the clutter, I found an old box of photos and letters. As we sifted through them, I came across a letter I'd written to myself years ago—long before my marriage, before Mikaela, before the challenges that shaped me.

The letter read:

"Dear Future Me,

I hope you've found the courage to love yourself as much as you love others. I hope you're living boldly and unapologetically. And most of all, I hope you're happy."

Tears filled my eyes as I read the words aloud.

"Wow, Mom," Mikaela said softly. "You've become everything you wanted to be."

In that moment, I realized she was right. I had come full circle—not just for myself, but for Mikaela, for every woman who has ever felt like she wasn't enough, and for the little girl I once was, who dared to dream of something more.

THE FULL CIRCLE EXPANDS

The letter from my past stayed with me for days. I couldn't stop thinking about the girl I used to be—and how much she would admire the woman I'd become. Still, despite how far I'd come, I knew my journey was far from over.

Mikaela's words echoed in my mind: "You've become everything you wanted to be." It was both humbling and empowering. Yet I felt a pull to keep going, to build something lasting. I wanted to create a legacy.

One evening, as I sat at my kitchen table with a steaming cup of tea, I began jotting down ideas for my next steps. *The Color of Pretty* conference was thriving, and my book was taking shape—but something was missing.

"What if I started a mentorship program?" I said aloud.

It felt obvious—almost overdue. Women reached out to me daily, sharing stories of overcoming insecurities, career hurdles, and personal struggles. Many asked for guidance. It was clear the next chapter of *Color of Pretty* needed to be a space for mentorship and growth.

The next morning, I called a meeting with my team and pitched the idea.

"I want to create a program where women of all ages can connect with mentors who look like them, understand their struggles, and can guide them toward success," I said, my voice brimming with excitement.

The team was immediately on board. Within weeks, we had a blueprint for the Pretty in Power mentorship program. It would pair mentors and mentees from all walks of life, fostering connection and building bridges across generations.

We got to work. *Pretty in Power* wasn't just about career advancement—it was about life, confidence, and breaking through the barriers that had held so many of us back for generations.

I envisioned a space where women could not only seek advice but form genuine, lasting connections with those who had walked similar paths. I wanted young women who doubted their worth to sit across from someone who had been in their shoes and hear the words, *"I see you. I was you. And you are going to be just fine."*

We began reaching out to industry leaders, entrepreneurs, educators, and changemakers—women who had shattered glass ceilings and forged their own paths. To my surprise, the response was overwhelming. So many wanted to give back, to share their journeys, lessons, victories, and even their failures.

The first *Pretty in Power* mentorship brunch was held in a bright, airy venue with floor-to-ceiling windows overlooking the city skyline. The energy in the room was electric. Women of all ages gathered, exchanging stories, laughter, and tears.

During my opening speech, I looked out at the crowd, my heart swelling with emotion.

"We are not just here to inspire; we are here to uplift, to guide, and to remind each other that we are capable of more than we ever imagined. Today is not just about mentorship—it's about sisterhood. Because when one of us rises, we all rise."

By the end of the event, mentor-mentee pairs had formed, and lifelong connections had begun.

As I watched women exchange numbers, embrace, and promise to stay in touch, I knew we had created something special.

That night, lying in bed and scrolling through messages from attendees sharing how transformative the event had been, I smiled to myself.

This wasn't just a movement anymore.

This was a legacy in the making.

A NEW LOVE

While my professional life was reaching new heights, my personal life took an unexpected turn.

On a crisp autumn afternoon, I attended a networking event for women in leadership. The event was inspiring, as always, but what caught me off guard was meeting someone who would change my life in ways I didn't expect.

His name was Malcolm, one of the event sponsors. As the owner of a nonprofit consulting firm, he focused on helping women-led organizations thrive. He was smart, kind, and carried himself with a quiet confidence that intrigued me.

"Lola Brown, right?" he said as he approached me during a break. "I've heard a lot about your work. The *Color of Pretty* conferences are incredible."

"Thank you," I said, surprised but flattered. "And Malcolm... Smith? Your nonprofit work is just as impressive."

We laughed and chatted, and before I knew it, we were deep in conversation—long after the event ended.

Over the next few months, we got to know each other better. Malcolm wasn't just supportive of my work; he was passionate about empowering others in ways that aligned with my mission. For the first time in a long time, I felt like I had found someone who truly understood me.

Dating Malcolm wasn't like anything I'd experienced before. No games, no insecurities, no doubts. He saw me for who I was— scars, triumphs, and all—and he celebrated it.

"Lola, you're a force," he said one evening as we walked through the park. "You don't just inspire people; you give them the tools to change their lives. That's rare."

His words stayed with me. For so long, I had fought to believe in myself. Now, here was someone who believed in me without hesitation.

Malcolm's presence in my life felt like a breath of fresh air— steady, reassuring, and filled with an ease I hadn't known before. He wasn't trying to fix me, and he wasn't intimidated by my ambition. He simply stood beside me, offering support that felt natural, not forced.

One evening, after a long day of meetings and planning for the next *Color of Pretty* event, he surprised me with dinner at my favorite restaurant.

"You need to take a break sometimes," he teased, handing me a glass of wine.

I chuckled, shaking my head. "Easier said than done. You know how much I have on my plate."

"That's exactly why you need someone to remind you that life isn't just about work." He leaned forward, his gaze serious yet warm. "You pour so much into others, Lola. Who's pouring into you?"

His words settled deep in my chest. For years, I had been the strong one—the fixer, the problem solver. I'd learned to rely on myself because depending on others so often led to disappointment. But Malcolm wasn't trying to take over my life—he was offering to walk beside me.

And that was something I wasn't used to.

As the months passed, Malcolm became more than a romantic partner; he became a true partner in every sense. When I needed advice, he listened. When I felt overwhelmed, he reminded me to breathe. When I doubted myself, he was there—steady and unwavering.

One night, as we sat on my couch, surrounded by paperwork and vision boards for my foundation's expansion, he reached over and took my hand.

"I know you're used to doing things alone, Lola. But you don't have to anymore. I'm here."

Tears pricked my eyes at the sincerity in his voice. I had spent so much time being strong that I hadn't realized how much I needed a safe place to land. And maybe, just maybe, Malcolm was that place.

For the first time in a long time, I allowed myself to believe in the possibility of love—not the kind I once chased, but the kind that found me when I wasn't even looking.

Chapter 4

LEGACY IN MOTION

> *"A legacy is built on the quiet moments*
> *where lives are changed."*

By the time the second *Color of Pretty* conference came around, the *Pretty in Power* mentorship program was in full swing. Hundreds of women had signed up as mentors and mentees, and stories of transformation were pouring in.

On the final day of the conference, I invited a few mentees to the stage to share their experiences.

"Before this program, I didn't know where to start," one young woman said, her voice trembling with emotion. "I felt lost, invisible, and unsure of my future. But my mentor didn't just guide me—she showed me that I had the strength to guide myself. Today, I'm starting my own business, and it's all thanks to this program."

The applause was thunderous. As I looked out at the audience, I saw tears, smiles, and nods of recognition.

"Ladies," I said, taking the microphone for the closing remarks, "this is why we're here. This is what it's all about. Together, we're breaking barriers, building bridges, and proving that we're stronger when we lift each other up. Let's keep doing the work. Let's keep creating spaces where every woman knows she is worthy, powerful, and pretty—inside and out."

The applause felt like waves of affirmation as I stepped off the stage. Malcolm was waiting backstage, his smile warm and reassuring.

"You did it again," he said, pulling me into a hug.

"No," I replied, smiling. "*We* did it."

The energy in the room was palpable. Women from all walks of life—entrepreneurs, students, mothers, and professionals—stood together, united by a shared purpose. *Color of Pretty* was no longer just a conference or a foundation; it was a movement.

After the event, attendees lingered—hugging, exchanging numbers, promising to stay connected. I watched friendships form in real time, women finding strength and solace in each other's stories.

Backstage, I took a deep breath, letting the moment sink in. This was what I had dreamed of: a space where women could show up as their full, unapologetic selves.

Malcolm squeezed my hand. "This is bigger than even you imagined, isn't it?"

I nodded, emotion rising in my chest. "It is. And it's only the beginning."

Over the next few months, the *Color of Pretty* Foundation expanded beyond anything I had envisioned. We launched mentorship chapters in multiple cities, partnered with schools to introduce self-esteem workshops, and secured funding to offer scholarships for young women pursuing their dreams.

One evening, as I sat in my office reviewing the latest impact reports, an email stopped me in my tracks.

Subject: Thank You for Changing My Life

Lola,

I don't know if you remember me, but I attended your first conference, and that day changed everything for me. I was in a dark place, unsure of my worth, questioning my future. But hearing you speak—hearing the stories of other women—made me realize I wasn't alone.

Because of Color of Pretty, I went back to school. I started believing in myself. I'm now the first in my family to graduate from college. I just wanted to say thank you—for seeing me when I couldn't see myself.

With gratitude,

Aisha

Tears blurred my vision as I read her words over and over.

This. This was why I started.

It was never about the stages, the applause, or the recognition. It was about impact. It was about making sure no woman ever felt invisible or unworthy.

I leaned back in my chair and exhaled deeply.

The work wasn't done—but I was ready.

The legacy had begun.

LOVE IN BLOOM

In the early months of my relationship with Malcolm, everything felt perfect. He was attentive, supportive, and fully invested in my work and my life. We took romantic weekend trips, stayed up late dreaming out loud, and seemed to bring out the best in each other.

Malcolm wasn't just a boyfriend—he was a partner. He volunteered at my events, introduced me to key people in his network, and even played an active role in *Pretty in Power*.

"You're my queen," he would say. "And I'll always stand by your side."

But over time, cracks began to form in the foundation of our seemingly perfect relationship.

THE SHIFT

At first, it was subtle. Malcolm began rescheduling dates, blaming last-minute work meetings. Then, his replies to my calls and texts grew slower, more indifferent. One evening, after a draining day of meetings, I called to vent about a sponsorship deal that had fallen through. "I'm just so frustrated," I said. "It feels like no matter how much progress we make, there's always a setback." There was a pause before he finally responded. "Lola, you're always stressed about work. Can't we just have a normal conversation that's not about your conferences or programs?" His words stung. My work wasn't just a job—it was my purpose. And Malcolm had always supported that. Or so I thought.

UNSPOKEN TENSIONS

The distance between us grew—both physical and emotional. Malcolm began canceling plans more often, and when we were together, he seemed distracted, constantly checking his phone or venting about his own work stress.

One night, over dinner, I decided to address the tension.

"Malcolm, is everything okay with us? You've seemed distant lately," I said, trying to keep my voice steady.

He sighed and set down his fork. "It's not that anything's wrong, Lola. It's just... you're so focused on your career and your events. Sometimes, I feel like there's no room for me in your life."

His words hit like a punch to the gut. I'd always seen us as a team, but now it felt like he was keeping score.

"Malcolm, my work is important to me—but so are you. If you're feeling neglected, we need to talk about it, not let it fester," I said, holding back tears.

He nodded, but the conversation felt unfinished.

REVELATIONS

The breaking point came a few months later. I had planned a weekend getaway for his birthday, but he canceled at the last minute, saying he needed to prepare for a major presentation.

That night, while scrolling through social media, I saw a photo that made my heart sink—Malcolm, tagged at a bar with colleagues, laughing and holding a drink.

I confronted him the next day.

"Why did you lie to me?" I asked, holding up my phone with the post on the screen.

He hesitated. "I didn't lie. I was with colleagues. It wasn't a big deal."

"But you said you had to work. I planned an entire weekend for us, Malcolm. Do you even care?"

His face tightened. "Lola, not everything revolves around you and your plans. Sometimes I need space, okay?"

THE BREAKING POINT

That argument marked a turning point in our relationship. The trust we had built began to crumble, and the warmth that once defined our bond gave way to resentment.

Malcolm started pulling away even more, and I found myself wondering if I was clinging to something that no longer served either of us.

One evening, after yet another canceled date, I sat down and wrote him a letter.

"Malcolm,

I love you, and I value the time we've spent together. But it feels like we're moving in different directions. I need someone who can support me as much as I support them—someone who sees my passion as a strength, not a burden. If that's not where you are, I understand, but I can't keep fighting for us alone."

When I handed him the letter, his expression was a mix of sadness and relief.

"I care about you, Lola," he said. "But maybe we're not as compatible as we thought."

HEALING AND GROWTH

Letting go of Malcolm was hard, but it was necessary. I realized I couldn't dim my light to make someone else comfortable, nor could I expect someone to align with my journey if their heart wasn't in it.

As I poured my energy back into my work and my own healing, I found solace in the women I had empowered through *Color of Pretty*. Their stories reminded me that every ending is also a chance for a new beginning. And while Malcolm's chapter in my life had closed, I knew my story was far from over.

HEALING THROUGH REFLECTION

After my relationship with Malcolm ended, I spent a lot of time reflecting on what went wrong—not just with him but within myself. I wasn't angry; I was heartbroken, but there was also clarity in the pain. I realized I had been bending and contorting myself to fit into his world while neglecting the space I had so carefully carved out for myself.

Therapy became my sanctuary again—not because I was broken, but because I wanted to remain whole. My therapist asked me a question that stuck with me: "Lola, do you love yourself as deeply as you want others to love you?"

I thought I did, but as I sat there, I realized my love for myself had limits. I had been putting conditions on my self-worth, tying it to how much I could give, how successful I could be, or how loved I felt in my relationships.

So, I started dating myself. I'd take myself out to dinner, go to art exhibits, and journal my thoughts like I was writing love letters to my soul. Slowly but surely, I began to feel like I was enough again—not because of what I achieved or who I was with, but simply because I existed.

Chapter 5

CONFIDENCE ON THE RISE

"For the first time in my life, I felt truly aligned. I wasn't just chasing success; I was living my purpose."

With stability in my personal life, my professional life began to soar. Color of Pretty was no longer just a conference—it had become a movement.

I launched a mentorship program for young women, pairing them with professionals across industries to help guide their journeys. We held workshops on self-esteem, financial literacy, and navigating career challenges.

The third *Color of Pretty* conference doubled in size. Sponsors began reaching out to me instead of the other way around. National publications requested interviews, and my inbox was filled with messages from women sharing how the movement had changed their lives.

One email stood out. It was from a young woman named Brianna, who had attended the first conference:

"Dear Lola,

I just wanted to thank you. I've struggled with feeling like I wasn't enough for so long, but hearing your story gave me hope. I've since started therapy, enrolled in school, and even applied for a job I never thought I could get. And guess what? I got it. Thank you for reminding me that confidence looks good on me."

Tears streamed down my face as I read her words. This was why I fought so hard—not just for myself, but for women like Brianna who needed someone to remind them of their worth.

As Color of Pretty grew, so did my vision. What began as a simple conference evolved into a full-fledged empowerment ecosystem, reaching women and girls across the country.

The mentorship program expanded beyond anything I had imagined. Executives, entrepreneurs, and trailblazing professionals signed up to guide young women on their paths. We partnered with corporations to offer internships, hosted financial literacy boot camps, and launched a leadership academy to prepare women for boardrooms, businesses, and beyond.

Demand for our work soared. Universities invited me to speak. Companies asked me to develop training programs focused on confidence and self-worth in the workplace. And then, something I never expected happened—major media outlets took notice.

A journalist from a leading women's magazine reached out, requesting an interview for a feature titled *Game Changers: Women Who Are Reshaping the Future*. Seeing my name in that lineup was surreal.

The interview took place in a bright, modern office in New York City. Cameras flashed as I sat across from the reporter, who smiled warmly. "Lola, your movement has changed lives. Did you ever imagine The *Color of Pretty* would become this big?"

I paused before answering. "Honestly? No. But I always knew the impact would be real. Because this isn't just about me—it's about every woman who's ever felt unseen, unheard, or unworthy. We're rewriting the narrative together."

A few weeks later, I was standing in line at a bookstore when my phone buzzed with a text from Mikaela: *Mom, check the magazine stands. You're on the cover!*

I nearly dropped my phone. Heart pounding, I rushed to the aisle—and there it was. My face, staring back at me, with the headline: *Lola Brown: Leading a Confidence Revolution.*

Tears welled in my eyes. It wasn't about fame or recognition. It was about the message.

I sent a silent prayer of gratitude.
For the girl I once was.
For the woman I had become.
For every woman still on her journey.

This was only the beginning.

FINDING BALANCE

As my career flourished, I made a promise to myself to maintain balance. I wasn't going to let my work consume me the way it once had. I carved out time for family, friends, and Darren, who had become my rock in the best way possible.

"Mikaela, you ready?" I called one Saturday morning as we packed up the car for her sophomore year of college.

"I can't believe you're driving me back," she teased. "Aren't you supposed to be this big, busy boss lady?"

"Even boss ladies take time for their babies," I replied, pulling her into a hug.

THE FUTURE AWAITS

One evening, as I sat in my new office now overlooking a bustling downtown skyline, I opened my journal and wrote down my next big idea: *The Color of Pretty Foundation.* I wanted to create scholarships, grants, and community centers to reach even more women and girls around the world.

For the first time in my life, I felt truly aligned. I wasn't just chasing success; I was living my purpose.

As I closed my journal and looked out at the city lights, I whispered the words that had carried me through it all:

"I am enough."

The more I wrote, the more the vision crystallized. I could see it all so clearly—the young girl walking into a Color of Pretty center for the first time, seeing herself in the mentors who would guide her. The single mother receiving a grant to start the business she had always dreamed of. The woman who had been told she wasn't *enough* finally realizing that she was more than enough.

Tears stung my eyes as I set my pen down. For the first time in my life, I felt truly aligned. *I wasn't just chasing success; I was living my purpose.*

MIKAELA'S GRADUATION: A PROUD MOMENT

Four years flew by faster than I ever imagined. It felt like just yesterday I was dropping Mikaela off at her dorm, fighting back tears as I gave her one last hug before she stepped into a new chapter of her life. Now, I sat in a packed auditorium, surrounded by proud parents, siblings, and friends, all waiting to hear their loved ones' names called.

The air buzzed with excitement—families cheered, cameras flashed, and graduates beamed with pride. My heart pounded as I scanned the stage, waiting for the moment her name would echo through the speakers. When it finally did, I jumped to my feet, clapping so hard my hands stung, cheering louder than anyone in the room.

There she was. My baby girl. My strong, resilient, brilliant daughter walking across that stage with a confidence that took my breath away.

Her cap, decorated in shimmering gold letters, read: *Strength Runs in My Veins.*

I let out a shaky breath, my chest tightening with emotion. Those words weren't just a statement—they were a testament to everything she had endured and overcome. She had turned every challenge, every setback, every hard-earned lesson into a stepping stone toward her future.

After the ceremony, I pushed through the crowd, searching for her. When our eyes met, she ran to me, and before I could speak, she pulled me into a tight hug.

"Mom, thank you," she whispered, her voice thick with emotion.

"For what?" I asked, cupping her face as I wiped away a tear.

"For never giving up on me. For showing me what strength looks like. For proving that no matter how hard life gets, we can rise. You're my inspiration."

I swallowed the lump in my throat and held her tighter. *She had no idea how much she had inspired me, too.*

I pulled back to look at her—my little girl, now a phenomenal young woman. "Mikaela, you did this," I said, my voice steady, filled with pride. "You worked for this. You fought for this. And this is just the beginning. The world has no idea what's coming."

We laughed through our tears, taking photos, sharing stories, and celebrating with friends and family. In that moment, every late-night talk, every hard conversation, every therapy session, and every sacrifice we made felt worth it.

As I watched my daughter—standing tall in her cap and gown, eyes full of dreams—I knew in my heart that this was just the beginning.

She was ready to take on the world. And I would always be right there, cheering her on.

TRAVELING WITH MY ROCK-SOLID TRIBE

Shortly after Mikaela's graduation, my phone buzzed with a call from Audra. Her voice crackled with excitement—the kind that meant she had something brewing.

"Lola, listen," she said, skipping the pleasantries. "It's time we did something for us. We've all been through so much these past few years—love, loss, growth, rebuilding. How about a girls' trip? Just us. No work, no distractions. Just friendship and fun."

The idea was met with instant enthusiasm. Latonya, our meticulous planner, dove into research, crafting the perfect mix of relaxation and adventure. Karen suggested Bali, raving about its tranquility, while Shelly, our wanderlust queen, pushed for Greece.

"Why choose?" I said, feeling a spark of joy. "Let's do both."

And just like that, our much-needed escape was set.

We started in Bali, checking into a stunning villa nestled in lush greenery, surrounded by infinity pools and the soothing hum of nature. Each morning began with sunrise yoga, led by a local instructor who taught us the power of stillness. We meditated by the ocean, letting the waves carry away years of stress.

Our afternoons were filled with exploration—wandering vibrant markets, indulging in spa treatments that felt like renewal, and visiting sacred temples where we prayed for clarity and continued blessings. Evenings were for laughter, long talks, and wine under open skies.

Karen kept us in stitches with her impressions and wild stories, while Shelly captured every moment on camera—the raw joy, the grateful tears, the quiet realization that we had all grown into the women we were always meant to be.

Then came Greece—a dream within a dream. We island-hopped across the Aegean Sea, the salty breeze tangling our hair as we sailed past whitewashed cliffs and cobalt waters. We danced barefoot under the stars in Mykonos, carefree and alive, as if the universe had choreographed that moment just for us.

We indulged in authentic Mediterranean cuisine, savoring every bite of grilled seafood, warm bread, and the richest olive oil we'd ever tasted. Late at night, over glasses of ouzo, we reflected on the journeys that brought us here—the heartbreaks that shaped us, the friendships that sustained us, and the dreams we were still bold enough to chase.

This trip wasn't just about where we went. It was about rediscovering who we were. It was a celebration of the women we'd become and the unbreakable bond that had carried us through every season of life.

One evening, standing on the cliffs of Santorini, watching the sun melt into the horizon in a blaze of orange and pink, Audra wrapped an arm around me and whispered, "Lola, we made it. Through everything—we made it."

And in that moment, with the ocean stretching endlessly before us and my best friends beside me, I felt it deep in my soul.

Yes, we had made it. And the best was still ahead.

TRUE FRIENDSHIPS, TRUE STRENGTH

Audra, Latonya, Karen, and Shelly had become more than just friends—they were my sisters. The kind of women who didn't just stand beside me in the sunshine but held umbrellas over me in the rain. Each had been a rock in different seasons of my life, showing up in ways only true friends could.

Audra was the voice of reason, the one who saw the angles I was too emotional to recognize. She didn't just offer advice; she made me think— deeply and critically—guiding me to look past immediate frustrations to the bigger picture. When I wanted to react, she reminded me to respond. Her wisdom was a steady hand, keeping me grounded when my emotions threatened to tip me over.

Latonya was the nurturer, the quiet force of comfort when life felt too heavy. She never asked, "Do you need anything?" because she already knew. She just showed up—whether it was with a home-cooked meal when I was too tired to think or a warm embrace when I had no words left. She spoke the language of love through action, proving that care wasn't about grand gestures but the simple act of being there.

Karen, my comedic relief, had a laugh that could shake a room. She made the impossible seem absurd and the unbearable feel temporary. Even in my darkest hours, she found a way to remind me that life was still worth smiling for. Her humor wasn't just a distraction—it was a reminder that joy could coexist with pain and that even on the hardest days, I could still find a reason to laugh.

And then there was Shelly—the dreamer, the believer. She saw potential in me that I often struggled to see in myself. Where I saw obstacles, she saw stepping stones. "You're bigger than this moment," she would say, refusing to let me settle for less than I deserved. She pushed me not just to survive but to thrive—to dream beyond my limitations and reach for things I once thought impossible.

Together, these women had carried me through heartbreaks, triumphs, failures, and victories. They had held my hand through grief, wiped my tears through disappointments, and celebrated every success, no matter how small. I learned that friendship wasn't just about the good times; it was about holding space for each other in the bad. It was about showing up, standing firm, and refusing to let go.

True friendship isn't measured by the moments of laughter but by the hands that hold you steady when the world is crumbling. It's not just about who walks in when times are good; it's about who refuses to walk away when they aren't.

And for these women—for their love, their loyalty, and their unwavering belief in me—I am endlessly grateful.

Chapter 6

A CITY OF DREAMS

"When the world feels overwhelming, remember: every skyscraper starts with a single brick, just like every dream begins with one bold step."

*B*ack home, Mikaela was preparing for her own adventure. She had accepted a job offer in New York City—a position she had worked tirelessly for, a dream she had nurtured for years. The moment had finally arrived, and while excitement buzzed in the air, so did the weight of change.

"Are you ready for the Big Apple?" I teased as we packed her things, folding memories between layers of clothes and wrapping love around each goodbye.

"Ready as I'll ever be," she said with a grin, though I could hear the nervous excitement in her voice. "But don't worry, Mom. I'll call every day."

I smiled, holding on to the promise, even though I knew how easily life could sweep people up in its whirlwind. As she loaded the last of her belongings into the car, I felt the familiar ache of motherhood—the joy of watching her soar mingled with the bittersweet pain of letting go.

I stood in the driveway, waving until her car disappeared down the road. My heart swelled with pride, but a quiet loneliness settled in. This was the moment every parent prepares for but never feels truly ready to face.

Still, I knew it was her time to shine, to step boldly into the life she had built for herself. So I took a deep breath, wiped a stray tear, and whispered to the wind, *Fly high, my girl. The world is yours now.*

The house felt different that evening—quieter, emptier. Her absence settled in like a soft echo, lingering in the stillness. I wandered into her room, half expecting to see her sitting on the bed, scrolling through her phone or humming along to one of her favorite songs. Instead, there were only remnants of her presence: an empty closet, a forgotten coffee mug on the nightstand, a childhood teddy bear she hadn't packed but couldn't quite bring herself to throw away.

I sat on the edge of her bed, running my hand over the comforter, remembering the little girl who once filled this space with laughter and dreams too big for this small town. Now, she was off chasing those dreams, stepping into the world she had always longed to be part of.

That night, I kept my phone close, just in case.

The next morning, as I was making coffee, my phone buzzed—a video call.

"Hey, Mom!" Mikaela's face filled the screen, her eyes bright, her smile reassuring. Behind her, the city skyline glowed with golden sunlight streaming through her apartment window.

"Hey, baby," I said, my heart instantly lighter. "You made it."

"I did," she said, glancing around. "And guess what? My apartment is tiny, my upstairs neighbor plays the trumpet at all hours, and I've already gotten lost twice." She laughed, shaking her head. "But it's amazing, Mom. I think I'm going to love it here."

I chuckled, wiping away a tear before she could see it. "I'm so happy for you, sweetheart."

And I was. Because in that moment, I realized she wasn't just my little girl anymore—she was a woman stepping into her own story, writing the next chapter of her life with courage and excitement.

No matter how far she went, I would always be her biggest fan, cheering her on from home.

REFLECTIONS AND GRATITUDE

One quiet evening after our trip, I sat on the porch with a cup of tea, reflecting on everything—Mikaela's graduation, the incredible journey we'd taken, and the women who had stood by me through it all.

Life wasn't perfect, but it was full, and I was grateful. I had come full circle—from a woman who once doubted her worth to one who had not only found it but shared it with others.

Looking up at the stars, I whispered a silent prayer of thanks—for Mikaela, for my tribe, and for the journey that had brought me here.

Because at the end of the day, life wasn't just about the hardships we endure—it was about the people who help us rise above them.

A few weeks after moving to New York City, Mikaela called during her lunch break, her excitement practically leaping through the phone.

"Mom! You won't believe it. I just met the CEO of my company in the elevator. She was so down-to-earth, and we ended up talking about the projects I'm working on. She even gave me a few tips on how to grow here."

"That's amazing, Mikaela!" I said, proud as ever. "How are you settling in otherwise?"

"I'm getting used to the city. It's a lot busier than Maryland, but I think I like the fast pace. And guess what? I found this cute little coffee shop near my apartment—it reminds me of home."

Hearing her excitement eased the ache of her absence. She told me about her job, her colleagues, and a new friend named Jamie, who had been showing her the ropes of city life.

As the months passed, Mikaela thrived. She sent pictures of her apartment, the skyline, and the events she attended. She was growing into her own person, carving out her path in a way that made me even more proud.

Back home, my friendship with Audra, Latonya, Karen, and Shelly continued to blossom. We started a tradition of monthly gatherings—sometimes at a local restaurant, sometimes at one of our homes. These weren't just casual get-togethers; they were healing.

One evening, we met at Latonya's house for a "vision board night." Armed with stacks of magazines, glue sticks, and a few bottles of wine, we spent hours cutting out images and words that spoke to our dreams.

"I'm focusing on wellness," Shelly said, holding up a picture of a serene beach. "I want to prioritize self-care this year."

"I'm all about career growth," Karen chimed in, holding up an image of a podium. "I want to land a big speaking gig."

As we worked on our boards, we shared stories, laughter, and a few tears. These moments reminded me how rare and beautiful it was to have friends who truly cared about my well-being.

One evening, Mikaela called, her voice more subdued than usual.

"Mom, I'm struggling," she admitted. "Work is intense, and I feel like I'm constantly trying to prove myself. It's overwhelming."

"Sweetheart, that's normal," I reassured her. "You're in a new city, in a demanding job. It's okay to feel this way. But remember, you're not alone. Lean on Jamie, call me anytime, and don't be afraid to ask for help."

Over time, Mikaela learned to navigate the challenges. She started journaling, practicing mindfulness, and attending networking events that helped her feel more connected. Each struggle became a stepping stone, and I watched her confidence grow with every step.

NEW ADVENTURES WITH MY TRIBE

One weekend, Karen, in true Karen fashion, decided we needed a break from life's routine. "We've been way too serious lately," she declared, hands on her hips like she was about to change our lives. "Let's just get in the car and go!"

No itinerary, no overthinking—just the open road and the four of us, ready for whatever adventure awaited.

Without much planning, we piled into Latonya's SUV, armed with snacks, oversized sunglasses, and a playlist full of throwback hits. The drive to Asheville, North Carolina, was pure joy—windows down, wind in our hair, and off-key karaoke that would've made record labels revoke our right to listen to music, let alone sing it.

By the time we arrived, we were buzzing with excitement. The Blue Ridge Mountains welcomed us with open arms, offering the kind of breathtaking views that made us pause in awe. We hiked trails that led to hidden waterfalls, stopped at roadside stands for homemade jams, and explored quirky little shops that smelled like cinnamon and nostalgia.

At a local pottery class, things took a hilarious turn. Karen, determined to craft something elegant, ended up with a lopsided bowl that vaguely resembled a deflated balloon. Shelly, after much concentration, held up her creation proudly.

"It's abstract art," she announced, tilting it slightly as if that would make it look intentional.

Audra, ever the perfectionist, somehow managed to shape a respectable vase, while Latonya spent most of the time wiping clay off her face, laughing too hard to focus.

By evening, we were gathered around a crackling campfire, bellies full from a feast of local barbecue and craft beer. The air was crisp, scented with pine and the lingering warmth of embers. Wrapped in blankets, I looked around at these incredible women— my sisters in every way that mattered.

"Ladies," I said, my voice thick with emotion, "you have no idea how much you mean to me. You've been my rock through everything, and I'm so grateful for you."

Audra, wise as always, smiled knowingly. "Lola, we've all been through our own storms. But the beauty of this friendship is that we weather them together."

And in that moment, under a sky full of stars, I knew there was no journey—no adventure, no hardship, no joy—I ever wanted to face without them by my side.

As the fire crackled and the night stretched on, our laughter softened into a comfortable silence—the kind that only happens between people who know each other's hearts and don't need to fill every moment with words. The stars above twinkled like tiny reminders that we were exactly where we were meant to be.

Karen poked at the fire with a stick, sending sparks drifting into the air. "We should make this a tradition," she said. "A girls' trip every year. No excuses."

Latonya raised her cup. "I second that!"

Shelly grinned. "And next time, I promise my pottery will be less… abstract."

We all laughed, knowing full well that wasn't going to happen.

As the embers glowed, we shared stories—some we'd told a hundred times, others we'd kept tucked away until now. We talked about the moments that shaped us, the love we had gained and lost, and the dreams we were still chasing.

Audra, ever the deep thinker, looked up at the sky. "You know, life moves so fast. We spend so much time worrying about what's next that we forget to enjoy where we are." She turned to me with a knowing smile. "Like right now, Lola. You're always looking ahead, planning the next thing. But tonight? Just be here."

Her words settled in my chest. She was right. I had spent so much of my life anticipating, fixing, and controlling. But here, with my best friends, surrounded by laughter and warmth, there was nothing to fix. Nothing to plan. Just a perfect moment, exactly as it was.

I took a deep breath, inhaling the cool mountain air, the scent of burning wood, the faint trace of pine. I let myself sink into the now, into the quiet joy of being with the people who had stood by me through every season of my life.

As the fire dimmed and we finally made our way into our cozy little cabin, I felt lighter. This trip had been exactly what I didn't know I needed.

The next morning, we packed up the SUV, but something had shifted. It wasn't just a weekend getaway—it was a promise. A reminder that no matter where life took us, we would always make time for each other.

As we drove away, the mountains fading in the rearview mirror, I smiled to myself. Life would keep moving. New challenges would come. But with these women by my side, I knew one thing for sure: I would never walk through it alone.

BRIDGING THE GENERATIONS

As Mikaela continued to grow in her career and independence, I made sure she stayed connected to my circle of friends—the women who had shaped me, lifted me, and walked beside me through every season of life. Whenever she came home, we'd invite her to our gatherings, where laughter flowed as freely as the wine and wisdom was shared as naturally as old stories.

One evening, as we sat around the table in my living room, Shelly leaned forward with a grin. "Mikaela, your mom talks about you all the time," she said, raising her glass in a playful toast. "You're her pride and joy."

Mikaela, never one for sentimentality, smiled as she reached for my hand. "She's mine too," she said simply, giving it a gentle squeeze.

Over time, Mikaela began to see my friends not just as my confidantes but as mentors. They took her under their wings, sharing stories of their own struggles and triumphs, offering career advice, life lessons, and the kind of encouragement that only comes from women who've lived it all.

Karen, ever the comedian, told her, "The working world is just like high school with paychecks. Stay sharp, keep your circle tight, and don't let anyone dull your shine."

Audra, always thoughtful, added, "Every job, every experience teaches you something—even the hard ones. Don't be afraid to take up space, Mikaela. You belong in every room you walk into."

Latonya, the nurturer, reminded her, "Make time for yourself. Work will always be there, but life moves fast. Don't forget to enjoy it."

Watching them pour into my daughter the same way they had poured into me was a full-circle moment. These women had been my lifeline through every challenge, every heartbreak, every success. Now, they were doing the same for Mikaela, reinforcing the lessons I had tried so hard to teach her on my own.

One night, after everyone had gone home, Mikaela sat beside me on the couch, tucking her legs beneath her the way she used to as a little girl.

"Mom," she said thoughtfully, "you have really incredible friends."

I smiled, brushing a strand of hair behind her ear. "I know. And now, so do you."

In that moment, I realized something beautiful: friendship isn't just about who walks with you through life—it's about who you can pass that love, wisdom, and strength down to. Mikaela wasn't just growing in her career; she was growing in her understanding of what it means to have—and to be—a strong, supportive woman.

And knowing she had my tribe to help guide her made letting go just a little bit easier.

Over the years, Mikaela didn't just see my friends as mentors—she became part of the sisterhood. She called Audra for career advice, turned to Latonya when she felt overwhelmed and laughed with Karen when she needed someone to lighten the mood. Shelly even took her out for coffee one afternoon and gave her a brutally honest talk about work-life balance.

"Let me tell you something, Mikaela," Shelly said, stirring her latte. "Climbing the ladder is great, but if you burn yourself out getting there, what's the point?"

That evening, Mikaela came home shaking her head. "Shelly doesn't hold back, does she?"

I laughed. "No, and that's why we love her."

It warmed my heart to watch Mikaela lean on them the way I had. It reminded me that true friendship—real, deep, soul-nurturing friendship—isn't meant for just one generation. It's meant to be passed down. It's meant to live on.

One holiday season, after a long dinner filled with stories and good wine, Mikaela turned to me as we did the dishes.

"Mom, I get it now," she said softly.

I looked at her, raising an eyebrow. "Get what?"

"This. All of it. The way you and your friends show up for each other, no matter what. I used to think friendships like yours were just luck—like you just happened to meet the right people at the right time." She set a plate on the drying rack and turned to face me. "But it's not luck, is it? It's a choice. You all choose to be there for each other. Over and over."

I set down my dish towel and pulled her into a hug, my heart swelling.

"That's exactly it, baby. Real friendships take work, but when you find your people, you hold on to them."

She smiled. "I hope I have friendships like yours one day."

"You will," I said. "Because now you know what to look for—and more importantly, you know how to be that kind of friend."

In that moment, I realized Mikaela wasn't just growing into her career or independence—she was becoming the kind of woman who understood the value of connection, support, and sisterhood. She had witnessed the power of true friendship firsthand, and I had no doubt she would one day have her own tribe, just as I had mine.

And that, more than anything, made me proud.

Chapter 7

UNVEILING YOUR POWER

"Transformation begins when you reclaim your own story."

With the third *Color of Pretty* conference behind me, I knew the fourth had to be even more impactful. The energy from the last event still lingered—women sharing stories of breakthroughs, renewed confidence, and healing. Some had found the courage to start new careers, leave toxic relationships, or finally prioritize themselves after years of neglect. That alone made all the sleepless nights of planning worth it.

But this time, I wanted to take the conference to another level. The theme I envisioned was *Unveiling Your Power.* It wouldn't be about fleeting motivation or temporary inspiration—it would be about transformation. About digging deeper, beyond surface-level insecurities, and helping women reclaim their narratives in ways that lasted long after the conference ended.

I spent months researching, curating speakers, and designing workshops to leave a lasting impact. I wanted this to be more than just another event—I wanted it to be a catalyst. A session on financial independence, a panel on mental health, and a keynote on breaking generational cycles were just a few of the ideas I jotted down. But I knew I needed my tribe to bring it all together.

As always, Audra, Latonya, Karen, and Shelly were right there with me, brainstorming and offering their expertise.

"You've got to add something about navigating relationships," Karen said one evening as we sat around my dining table, notebooks and laptops scattered across the surface. "Romantic, familial, friendships—it's all connected to how we see ourselves."

"Agreed," Shelly chimed in. "And don't forget self-care. Too many women think taking care of themselves is selfish when, really, it's survival."

Audra nodded thoughtfully. "What about a session on overcoming imposter syndrome? So many of us are walking around doubting our brilliance, waiting for someone to validate what we already know deep down."

Latonya, ever the nurturer, leaned forward. "And faith. No matter what someone believes in, there has to be a conversation about faith, resilience, and trusting the process."

Their insights were invaluable. They always helped me see the bigger picture and pushed me to go beyond what I thought was possible.

As the weeks passed, the pieces started coming together. I secured powerhouse speakers from different walks of life, each with a story to tell. We found a venue that felt like the perfect space for transformation, and I worked tirelessly to create an experience that wouldn't just inspire but equip women with the tools to truly step into their power.

One night, as I sat alone reviewing the agenda, I felt something stir in me—a deep knowing that this wasn't just another event. It was part of my purpose. Part of something bigger than me.

I closed my laptop and whispered to myself, "This is going to change lives."

And deep down, I knew I was right.

A NEW FACE, A NEW CONNECTION

Planning the conference took up most of my time, but life had a way of slipping in the unexpected. One evening, after a long strategy meeting with my team, I treated myself to dinner at a cozy bistro downtown—the kind of place with dim lighting, soft jazz, and an ambiance that invited you to stay awhile.

Notebook in hand, I planned to jot down ideas over a glass of wine. The conference was still on my mind, but more than anything, I just wanted to breathe and enjoy my own company without a schedule dictating my every move.

As I scanned the menu, a voice broke my thoughts.

"Excuse me, is this seat taken?"

I looked up, surprised. A tall man stood before me—confident, kind-eyed, his smile warm and unforced. Something about him made me pause.

"No, it's not," I said, caught slightly off guard but intrigued.

He introduced himself as Derrick, a business consultant new to the area. "I hate eating alone," he said with a chuckle. "But I promise I won't interrupt your work."

What began as a shared table became an unexpectedly engaging conversation. Derrick was sharp, funny, and easy to talk to. He asked about *The Color of Pretty* and seemed genuinely impressed.

"You're empowering women to see their worth," he said, thoughtful. "That's powerful. What inspired you?"

I hesitated, then shared a condensed version of my story—my struggles with self-worth, the painful marriage I'd overcome, and the moment I realized my journey could help others.

By the end of the evening, Derrick leaned back and smiled. "You've got something special, Lola. I'd love to hear more over coffee, maybe?"

"Strictly professional, of course," he joked, though his eyes said otherwise.

I agreed—maybe out of curiosity, or maybe because, for the first time in a long while, I'd met a man who seemed drawn to the substance of who I was.

As Derrick and I started spending more time together, I realized how refreshing it was to be with someone who wasn't intimidated by my ambition. He didn't shy away from conversations about my goals or minimize the work I was doing. Instead, he asked questions, listened intently, and celebrated my wins like they were his own.

But I was cautious. After everything I'd been through, I wasn't about to lose myself in someone else's world. I made it clear that Mikaela and my work were my priorities.

"Understood," Derrick said one evening over coffee. He didn't flinch, didn't try to convince me otherwise. He simply nodded, his expression sincere. "I'm not here to complicate your life, Lola. I just want to be a part of it however you'll let me."

His patience, his respect—it was a kind of gentleness I hadn't experienced in a long time. And while I wasn't sure where this would lead, I knew one thing for certain.

For the first time in years, I was open to finding out.

Days turned into weeks, and Derrick remained consistent. He didn't push, didn't try to rush anything. He was just there, showing up in small but meaningful ways. A morning text wishing me a great day. A call to check in after an exhausting meeting. An invitation to try a new coffee shop when he knew I needed a break from planning.

I hadn't realized how much I'd been bracing myself for disappointment, waiting for the other shoe to drop. But Derrick wasn't playing a game. He was simply present.

One evening, after a particularly long day, he called.

"Busy?" he asked.

"Always," I sighed, rubbing my temples. "But I could use a distraction."

"Perfect," he said. "Come outside."

Confused, I walked to my front door and opened it to find him standing on my porch, holding two takeout bags and wearing that same easy smile.

"I figured you probably forgot to eat," he said with a shrug. "And I make it a personal mission never to let people suffer through bad takeout decisions."

I laughed a real, full-bodied laugh that I hadn't felt in days. "You don't even know what I like."

"True, but I took a risk. Thai food. Hope I guessed right."

He did.

We sat on my couch, eating straight from the containers, talking about everything and nothing. For the first time in ages, I let myself enjoy the moment—no overthinking, no questioning what it meant or where it might lead.

"I like this," I said after a pause, surprising even myself.

Derrick raised an eyebrow. "The food?"

I shook my head. "This. The simplicity. No expectations, no pressure. Just... good company."

He set down his fork, his expression serious but warm. "That's all I want, Lola. I don't need anything from you. I just want to know you."

And for the first time in a long while, I believed him.

I didn't know what this was or what it could become, but I wasn't afraid of it.

For the first time in years, I wasn't just surviving—I was letting myself live.

THE FOURTH CONFERENCE: A MILESTONE

The day of the fourth *Color of Pretty* conference finally arrived. The venue buzzed with energy as over 2,000 women filled the space. The workshops were a hit, the speakers were inspiring, and the atmosphere was electric.

Backstage, moments before my keynote, I spotted Mikaela in the front row, beaming with pride. Beside her were Audra, Latonya, Karen, and Shelly—the women who had been my backbone through every season of life.

I took a deep breath and stepped onto the stage. "Welcome, everyone, to the fourth annual *Color of Pretty* conference. Today, we celebrate resilience, power, and the beauty of being unapologetically you."

The crowd erupted in applause, and for a moment, I felt like I was floating.

That evening, as I mingled with attendees, Derrick appeared. "You were incredible up there," he said, handing me a bouquet of sunflowers. "I'm proud of you."

With the fourth conference behind me and a budding relationship with Derrick, it felt like a new chapter was beginning. My friendships were stronger than ever, Mikaela was thriving in her career, and I was finally open to love again.

Later that night, surrounded by notes and plans for what's next, I sat in my living room with a quiet sense of peace. Life wasn't perfect, but it was beautiful in its own way.

EXPLORING LOLA & DERRICK'S RELATIONSHIP

At first, I approached my connection with Derrick cautiously, like someone testing the water's temperature before diving in. He was kind, attentive, and patient—qualities I hadn't consistently experienced in past relationships. Still, after years of healing and self-discovery, I'd learned not to rush into anything that didn't align with my renewed sense of self-worth.

Our dates were simple but meaningful. Derrick had a way of making even the most mundane activities feel special. One Sunday afternoon, he suggested we visit a local farmers market.

"Fresh flowers, good food, and local artists—what's not to love?" he said with a grin.

We wandered through the aisles, sampling honey, browsing handmade jewelry, and admiring colorful bouquets. At one point, he handed me a small sunflower arrangement and said, "These reminded me of you. Bright, beautiful, and impossible to ignore."

I was taken aback by his thoughtfulness. "You're smooth, Derrick," I teased, though my smile gave away how much his words meant.

As our connection deepened, so did my fear of fully opening up. One evening, over dinner at my condo, Derrick noticed my hesitation.

"You seem distracted," he said, setting down his fork. "What's on your mind?"

I hesitated, then took a deep breath. "It's just... I've been through a lot. And as much as I enjoy spending time with you, part of me is scared—scared that if I let my guard down, I'll get hurt again."

Derrick reached across the table and took my hand. "Lola, I can't promise I'll never make mistakes, but I can promise I'll always be honest with you. You've been through fire and come out stronger. I'm not here to dim your light—I want to help it shine brighter."

His words felt like a balm on wounds I hadn't realized still ached.

Derrick was eager to meet Mikaela, but I was cautious about bringing him into her life. She'd seen me go through so much pain, and I didn't want her to feel like I was rushing into something new.

"Mom, I trust you," Mikaela said one evening after I voiced my concerns. "If you think Derrick is good for you, I'll support it. Just make sure he's as amazing as you deserve."

When they finally met, it was over brunch at one of Mikaela's favorite spots. To my relief, they hit it off almost immediately. Derrick asked thoughtful questions about her college experience and shared stories from his own upbringing, making her laugh with his self-deprecating humor.

As we walked back to the car, Mikaela leaned over and whispered, "I like him. He's... different."

"Different how?" I asked.

"In a good way. He seems like he actually sees you, Mom."

No relationship is without its challenges, and ours was no exception. Balancing work, relationships, and personal growth wasn't always easy. There were moments when I questioned whether I had space in my life for romance.

But Derrick never pressured me. "We're building something here," he said during one of our late-night talks. "And anything worth building takes time."

One particular hurdle came when an old insecurity resurfaced. We were at a networking event when a strikingly beautiful woman approached Derrick, laughing and resting a hand on his arm as they talked.

Though I knew it was harmless, I felt a familiar pang of doubt. That old voice whispered, *What if he realizes you're not enough?*

Later, as we drove home, I voiced my feelings. "Derrick, I trust you, but sometimes my past gets the better of me."

He pulled the car over and turned to me. "Lola, you are more than enough. And if I ever do something to make you feel otherwise, call me out on it. I don't want you carrying that weight alone."

As months passed and a year unfolded, our relationship deepened. Derrick became more than a partner—he became my cheerleader, encouraging me to take *The Color of Pretty* to new heights.

"You inspire so many people, Lola," he said one evening as I prepared for a speaking engagement. "But don't forget to let people inspire you, too. That's how you keep growing."

His words stayed with me. For the first time in a long time, I felt like I was part of a true partnership—one where we poured into each other equally.

LOOKING AHEAD

With the fourth *Color of Pretty* conference complete and Mikaela thriving in her own journey, life felt full in the best way. Derrick and I weren't perfect, but we were building something real—something worth holding onto.

One evening, as we sat on my balcony watching the sunset, Derrick turned to me. "Do you ever think about what's next?"

I smiled, leaning into his shoulder. "All the time. But for now, I'm just enjoying the moment."

And for the first time in a long time, I truly was.

THE GOOD, THE BAD, AND THE UGLY

In many ways, Derrick felt like the answer to a prayer I had whispered into the universe on countless lonely nights. He was everything I had hoped for—attentive, loving, protective, and steadfast. He cared for me in ways I hadn't realized I needed, and his presence was a balm to my soul. But as much as he lifted me up, a shadow began to creep into our relationship, casting an uncertain pall over our future: his drinking.

Derrick was my rock. Whether helping me plan the next conference, surprising me with my favorite flowers after a long day, or simply listening when I needed to vent, he had a way of making me feel seen and valued.

He was also wonderful with Mikaela. Whenever she came home from college, he made it a point to engage with her—offering advice, joking around, making her laugh. She told me once, "Mom, I like how he treats you. It's like he's making up for all the times you didn't have someone in your corner."

I couldn't deny it. Derrick made me feel safe, cherished, and deeply loved.

But there were nights when that warmth was overshadowed by the sting of reality. His drinking, something I had first brushed off as "just enjoying a good time," began to spiral into something harder to ignore.

At first, it was subtle—a few too many drinks at dinner, a slurred word, a forgotten conversation. But over time, the signs became unmistakable. He'd stumble in late at night, the scent of alcohol clinging to him like an unwanted guest.

"Derrick, are you okay?" I'd ask, concern tightening my voice.

"Relax, Lola. I'm fine," he'd reply, brushing me off with a wave of his hand.

His dismissiveness hurt more than I wanted to admit. I wasn't angry—I was worried.

One night, after an especially long day, Derrick came home visibly intoxicated. He was irritable and short-tempered, snapping at me over nothing.

"Why do you always have to nag, Lola? I'm working my ass off for us, and all you do is criticize," he said, his voice rising.

I stood there, stunned. This wasn't the Derrick I knew—the man who held me when I cried, who encouraged me to chase my dreams, who made me feel like the most important person in the world.

"I'm not criticizing, Derrick. I'm worried about you," I said softly, trying to de-escalate the moment.

He sighed, running a hand through his hair. "I'm sorry," he muttered, voice breaking. "I just... I don't know how to deal with everything sometimes."

That admission broke my heart. It wasn't just the alcohol—it was the weight he carried: the pressure to provide, to protect, to be everything he thought I needed.

After that night, I knew we had to face it head-on.

"Derrick, I love you," I said one evening as we sat on the couch. "But your drinking—it's starting to affect us. And I don't want to lose what we have."

He looked at me, eyes filled with guilt and vulnerability. "I know I've been drinking too much. I guess I've been using it as a crutch. But I don't want to lose you either, Lola. I'll do better—I promise."

It wasn't the first time he'd said it, but something in the way he held my hand made me believe he meant it this time.

We agreed to take steps together. Derrick began seeing a counselor, and I joined him for a few sessions. We set boundaries— no drinking during the week and a limit of one or two drinks at social events.

It wasn't easy. There were setbacks—nights when the stress pushed him back into old habits. But there were also victories. For example, when he came home after a rough day and said, "I wanted to stop at the bar, but I came straight home instead. Because I knew being here with you would make me feel better."

Those moments reminded me why I was fighting for us.

Derrick's journey with alcohol wasn't a straight line—it was a winding road of setbacks and growth. But through it all, he remained the man who loved me fiercely, who made me laugh, who stood by me no matter what.

"I'm not perfect, Lola," he said one night as we lay in bed. "But I'm trying. For you. For us."

"And that's all I can ask for," I replied, squeezing his hand.

I realized love isn't about finding someone flawless—it's about finding someone willing to grow, to fight for the relationship when things get hard.

Derrick wasn't just my partner; he was my reminder that life, like love, is messy and imperfect—but worth every moment.

Chapter 8

THE PROPOSAL THAT CHANGED EVERYTHING

"Love isn't about being perfect, it's about choosing each other every day, even when it's hard."

It was a crisp fall evening when Derrick proposed. We were at the park where we'd had one of our first dates—leaves scattered in shades of gold and red, a cool breeze dancing through the air. He'd been unusually quiet all day, stealing glances at me with a nervous energy I couldn't quite place.

"Lola," he began, as we stood by the lake, "being with you has been the greatest blessing of my life. You make me want to be better, to do better. I know I'm not perfect, and I know I've given you reasons to doubt me. But I also know I want to spend the rest of my life proving how much you mean to me."

Before I could fully process his words, he dropped to one knee and pulled out a small velvet box.

"Lola Brown, will you marry me?"

Time seemed to freeze. My heart raced as I stared down at him, his eyes full of hope and vulnerability.

I opened my mouth to respond, but no words came. Instead, a flood of emotions washed over me—joy, fear, love, doubt.

Was I ready for this? Could I truly commit to a man with struggles, knowing they might resurface? Was I setting myself up for heartbreak again?

My mind drifted to my past—Trey's betrayal, the years I spent feeling unworthy of love, the battles I fought to reclaim my sense of self. I had worked hard to build a life that didn't revolve around someone else.

"Lola, say something," Derrick said softly, his voice cutting through the chaos.

"I... I don't know," I whispered, tears welling in my eyes. "Derrick, I love you. I really do. But marriage? It's a lot. And honestly, I'm scared."

He stood and took my hands. "I know, Lola. I know your fears because I see them. But I also see your strength, your resilience, your heart. I don't want to rush you. I just need you to know I'm here for the long haul—however long it takes."

Over the next few weeks, I wrestled with the decision. I confided in Latonya, who was visiting.

"Lola, I've seen you at your lowest, and I've seen you rise above it all," she said. "Derrick isn't perfect, but no one is. What matters is how he treats you and how willing he is to grow with you. But you have to be honest with yourself—can you see him as your partner for life?"

Her words lingered. Could I see Derrick as my forever? Despite his flaws, I could. Time and again, he'd shown he was willing to put in the work—for himself and for us.

One evening, as we sat on the couch watching a movie, I turned to him and said, "Derrick, about your question..." His eyes widened, his body tensing in anticipation. "Yes. I'll marry you," I said, a small smile spreading across my face.

Relief and joy washed over him as he pulled me into a tight embrace. "You won't regret this, Lola," he whispered. "I promise."

The weeks that followed were a whirlwind of emotions and celebration. We held an intimate engagement party with close friends and family. Mikaela gave a speech that brought tears to my eyes.

"To my mom," she said, raising her glass. "A woman who's taught me what it means to be strong, to love yourself, and to never settle for less than you deserve. And to Derrick—thank you for being the man who makes her smile like I haven't seen in years. Cheers to both of you."

As happy as I was, moments of doubt still crept in. What if I wasn't cut out for marriage? What if the drinking became a bigger issue? What if I failed again?

One night, I finally voiced my fears to Derrick. "Marriage isn't about having all the answers, Lola," he said. "It's about choosing each other every day, even when it's hard. I choose you. Always."

Each morning, as I slipped on my engagement ring, it reminded me of the commitment we were making—not just to each other, but to ourselves. It wasn't about being perfect. It was about being present, about showing up even when it wasn't easy.

Planning the wedding became a new adventure. Derrick was deeply involved, surprising me with his attention to detail and his excitement about the life we were building.

Through it all, I held onto one belief: love, in its truest form, isn't about avoiding challenges. It's about facing them head-on, hand in hand. And with Jordan, I was ready to do just that.

PLANNING THE PERFECT (COMPROMISED) WEDDING

Derrick and I approached wedding planning from two completely different worlds. I'd already done the grand affair—200 guests, elaborate decorations, a string quartet, and top-tier caterers. It had been a spectacle, a whirlwind of planning and stress. Though perfect on the outside, it lacked the love and intimacy I now craved.

Derrick, on the other hand, had experienced the opposite. His first wedding was a simple courthouse ceremony—no fanfare, no celebration, not even a photo to mark the day. This time, he wanted something entirely different: a church wedding his parents and three daughters could witness, something he could dedicate to God and his love for me.

At first, I pitched the idea of a destination wedding—a beautiful beach, the sound of waves as we exchanged vows, just a small circle of close friends and family. Derrick listened, then gently shook his head.

"Lola, I get it. I do. But I've never had a real wedding, and I want my girls to see this. I want them to see me get married the right way, in front of God, in a church."

I saw the conviction in his eyes. And while I still dreamed of an intimate, sandy ceremony, I knew this meant something deeper to him. So we compromised: a small, intimate church wedding.

Well, that's how it started.

The "small, intimate" wedding quickly grew into something else. Our original guest list of 50 crept up to 100.

"Lola, we can't leave out Aunt Desi," Derrick would say. "And what about my cousins from Atlanta?" I'd counter.

Soon, we were planning a mid-sized wedding. It wasn't the extravagance of my first, but it was enough to give me a few sleepless nights.

If there was one thing about Derrick, it was his frugality. He didn't see the point in spending $10,000 on flowers or renting an upscale venue when the local community center was available for half the price.

"I get it, Derrick, but you know how I am," I said, frustration slipping into my voice during one of our many budget talks. "I don't do cheap."

He raised his hands in mock surrender. "Okay, okay. But do we really need an ice sculpture?!"

"Maybe not," I admitted. "But we're not cutting corners on the photographer or the food. And absolutely no folding chairs with those tacky covers."

Despite the occasional clash over the budget, we found ways to make it work. Our church was beautiful but modest, requiring little decoration, which let us splurge on florals for the reception. I convinced Derrick that hiring a professional caterer was non-negotiable, and he saved us money by recruiting a friend to DJ.

Planning became an exercise in compromise—his practicality balanced my desire for elegance.

Derrick's daughters were thrilled to be part of the wedding. The oldest, Shayla, would be one of my bridesmaids, while the younger two, Laila and Kyra, were ecstatic to be flower girls.

"I've never seen my dad so happy," Shayla confided one afternoon as we shopped for dresses. "You're really good for him, Ms. Lola."

Her words warmed my heart and reminded me why this wedding mattered—not just for us but for the family we were creating together.

When the day finally arrived, all the stress and compromises melted away. The church was filled with our closest friends and family, soft music played, and Derrick's girls beamed as they walked down the aisle.

Standing at the back of the church, bouquet in hand, I took a deep breath and felt a wave of peace wash over me. This wasn't the grand affair I'd once imagined, but it was perfect in its own way.

When I reached Derrick at the altar, his eyes brimmed with tears. "You look stunning," he whispered.

"And you look like you're about to cry," I teased, though my own eyes glistened.

The reception was full of laughter, dancing, and heartfelt toasts. It wasn't my dream beach wedding, but it was ours—full of love, compromise, and the promise of a new beginning.

Later that night, as we sat together, exhausted but happy, I turned to Derrick. "You were right about one thing."

"What's that?" he asked.

"This was the right way to do it."

And for the first time in a long time, I felt like I was exactly where I was meant to be.

A HONEYMOON TO REMEMBER

Derrick and I wanted our honeymoon to be something special—something that reflected the love and joy we had built together. After all the stress of planning the wedding, we settled on a cruise: the perfect blend of relaxation, adventure, and quality time. But this wasn't going to be an ordinary honeymoon. We invited a few of our closest friends and their spouses, turning it into a celebration of love, friendship, and life.

Latonya and Ryan, Audra and DJ were all in. As soon as we told them the plan, they couldn't pack fast enough. "A cruise honeymoon with the squad? Say less!" Audra exclaimed, already planning matching outfits for our group excursions.

The moment we stepped onto the ship, the excitement was infectious. The sun was shining, the ocean stretched endlessly around us, and the possibilities felt infinite. From the start, we made it our mission to soak up every moment.

Derrick and I had a beautiful suite with a balcony overlooking the water, where we'd sit in the evenings and toast to the start of our new chapter. During the day, we were with our friends, exploring everything the ship had to offer.

Our first stop was the Dominican Republic, and it was breathtaking. We spent the day lounging on pristine beaches, sipping rum cocktails, and savoring the local food. Latonya, ever the adventurous one, convinced us to go zip-lining through the lush forests.

"I'm not sure about this!" Ryan shouted as he clung to his harness.

"Don't chicken out now!" Latonya yelled back, already soaring through the trees like a pro.

By the end of the day, we were sun-kissed and happy, with more than enough stories to laugh about over dinner back on the ship.

BELIZE ADVENTURES

Belize was a highlight for everyone. We signed up for a group snorkeling excursion that left us in awe of the vibrant marine life. Derrick and DJ turned it into a friendly competition to see who could dive the deepest.

"Did you see that stingray?!" Derrick asked, pulling off his mask as he resurfaced. "And that school of fish!" DJ replied.

Audra and I floated nearby, laughing at their antics while taking in the beauty of the coral reef. Later, we wandered through the charming town, indulging in local delicacies and picking up souvenirs for our families.

ST. THOMAS ELEGANCE

Our final stop was St. Thomas, and it was pure paradise. We booked a private catamaran tour and spent the day sailing, swimming, and toasting with chilled champagne. "This is the life," Ryan said, leaning back with a satisfied grin as the catamaran glided over turquoise waves.

Derrick pulled me close, and we watched the sun dip below the horizon. "I could get used to this," he said softly—and I couldn't help but agree.

Back on the ship, the fun didn't stop. We danced the night away at themed parties, tried our luck at the casino, and laughed until our stomachs hurt over dinner. Latonya and I even convinced the guys to join us for karaoke night. Their rendition of "My Girl" was equally adorable and hilarious, and by the end, the whole lounge was on its feet, clapping along.

This trip wasn't just about Derrick and me—it was about celebrating the love and friendship that had carried us through so much. Latonya and Ryan, Audra and DJ—they were more than friends; they were family. Having them there made everything more special. "This trip has been amazing," Audra said one evening as we all gathered on the deck under a blanket of stars. "It's been perfect," I replied, squeezing Derrick's hand.

When the cruise ended, none of us were ready to leave. The memories we'd made exploring new places, laughing until we cried, and simply being present with the people we loved were priceless.

As Derrick and I unpacked at home, I looked at him and smiled. "We couldn't have started this chapter any better." He kissed my forehead. "Here's to many more adventures, Mrs. Thompson." And with that, I knew our journey was only just beginning.

Chapter 9

MERGING LIVES, MANAGING LOVE

"Marriage isn't just about love; it's about teamwork, trust, and learning to build a future together."

After the excitement of the wedding and our unforgettable honeymoon, Derrick and I knew it was time to focus on the practical side of blending our lives. Marriage wasn't just about love and romance—it was about building a strong foundation for our future.

The first big decision was selling my condo. Letting go of the home I'd worked so hard to buy wasn't easy, but Derrick and I had a plan: I would move into his house, and after the holidays, we'd start looking for a new home together—something that would be ours from the ground up.

"Are you sure about this?" I asked one evening as we sat in the living room, surrounded by boxes of my things.

"I'm positive," he said, taking my hand. "This is just the beginning. We'll build something beautiful together."

With the move underway, we turned to the less glamorous—but equally important—tasks of marriage. We met with a financial advisor to merge our finances and set long-term goals. Combining bank accounts was a big step, especially since we'd both been independent for so long.

"I'm trusting you not to touch my shoe fund," I joked as we signed the paperwork. "Only if you don't raid my gadget fund," Derrick replied with a grin.

We also updated our life insurance policies and beneficiaries. It was a sobering moment, but we both understood the importance of protecting each other and our families.

"This isn't just about us," Derrick said. "It's about making sure our loved ones are taken care of—no matter what."

As the holidays approached, our home became a hub of activity. Derrick's three daughters filled the house with laughter and energy. They were thrilled to see their dad so happy and excited about the future.

"I've never seen Dad this excited about Christmas," his oldest daughter teased.

"Well, I'm a little extra," I said, adjusting a ribbon on the tree with a smile.

Derrick's family welcomed me with open arms, and I felt an overwhelming sense of belonging—a sharp contrast to the quiet holidays I'd spent alone in the past.

Of course, there were challenges. Our different approaches to money surfaced during conversations about the new house. "I want us to stay within a reasonable budget," Derrick said one evening. "We don't need anything extravagant."

"Derrick, you know I don't do 'cheap,'" I replied, only half-joking. "This is our forever home. I want it to feel special."

It took some back-and-forth, but we found common ground—a budget that allowed for the home of our dreams without overextending ourselves. "Marriage is about compromise, right?" Derrick said with a wink.

"Right," I replied, smiling. "But don't forget who you married. I like nice things."

As the new year began, I felt a sense of excitement and purpose. Selling my condo, moving in with Derrick, and tackling the logistics of married life had been challenging but also deeply rewarding.

Our love wasn't just in the big moments—the wedding, the honeymoon, the holidays. It lived in the day-to-day decisions, the compromises, and the quiet promises to build something lasting.

Looking at Derrick as we sat down to review potential homes, I felt a surge of gratitude.

"We're doing this," I said.

"We are," he replied, pulling me close. "And it's going to be amazing."

Two months into our marriage, we were eager to start the next chapter: finding the perfect home. But the timing couldn't have been worse. The housing market was chaotic—prices were sky-high, inventory was low, and every house we liked seemed to go under contract within hours.

"Is this what buying a home is like now?" I groaned after our third open house in one weekend.

"It's insane," Derrick agreed, rubbing his temples. "We're competing with people paying cash. How do we beat that?"

After weeks of frustration, we decided to pause and rethink our plan.

What if we transformed Derrick's house into our dream home instead?

A BAD EPISODE

The decision to renovate instead of buy wasn't the only challenge we faced in those first few months. One evening, after an especially stressful day at work, Derrick came home and started drinking. What began as a couple of beers quickly spiraled into something more troubling.

I found him in the living room, slurring his words and clearly upset. "Derrick," I said gently, trying to read his mood, "what's going on?" "Nothing," he muttered, avoiding my eyes. "Just needed to take the edge off." But it wasn't just that. This was deeper—and it scared me. The next morning, I brought it up.

"Derrick, last night wasn't okay," I said, sitting across from him at the kitchen table. "I love you, but we can't ignore this."

He stared into his coffee, shame flickering across his face. "You're right," he said quietly. "I've been under a lot of pressure, but that's not an excuse. I'll do better."

With the market still a mess, we decided to find a contractor to help reimagine Derrick's home. It was a compromise—he was attached to the house, and I wanted something that felt like "ours." If we couldn't find a new place, we'd make this one work.

The contractor was thorough and full of ideas, but the process came with hiccups. "You want to knock down that wall? That's going to be pricey," he said during the walkthrough. "Derrick, this is why we should've just kept looking for a new house," I said, exasperated.

"And spend how much more?" he snapped. "This is the smarter choice."

The tension between us was constant. We were both fiercely independent, and neither of us had lived with a partner in years. Finding our rhythm under the same roof was harder than we expected.

"Can we just pause for a second?" I said during one heated discussion. "This isn't about the house. It's about us learning how to work together."

Derrick let out a breath and nodded.

"You're right. I'm sorry. I'm not used to someone else's opinion in my space—but that's not fair to you. This is your home, too."

Despite the challenges, there were bright moments that reminded me why I chose him. Late-night talks about our future. His hand on my back when I felt overwhelmed. The way he made me laugh even when I wanted to scream.

"You're stuck with me, you know," he said one night as we flipped through paint samples.

"Good," I replied, leaning into him. "Because I'm not going anywhere."

As we navigated the ups and downs—contractors, his struggle with drinking, learning to share space—we started to find our groove. It wasn't perfect, but it was ours.

"Marriage isn't about perfection," I told him one evening after yet another argument about budget versus design. "It's about choosing each other every day, even when it's hard."

And we did. Every day, we chose each other.

THE HIDDEN STRUGGLE

While we tried to focus on renovating the house, a deeper issue was brewing: Derrick's drinking.

It started small: a glass of whiskey after work, a beer during a game. But gradually, it became more frequent and more intense. One night, I found him slumped on the couch, a half-empty bottle on the table, his words slurred and his tone distant.

"Derrick," I said softly, trying to hide the worry in my voice. "Is everything okay?"

"Yeah, I'm fine," he muttered, brushing me off.

But I wasn't fine. Seeing him like that stirred up memories I didn't want to revisit—feelings of rejection, fear, and uncertainty. I wanted to confront him, to tell him how much it scared me, but I didn't. Instead, I swallowed my feelings and smiled the next morning like nothing had happened.

I didn't know who to talk to. My friends—the women who had always been my rock—seemed like the obvious choice. But how could I admit to them, the same women who admired my strength, that I was struggling? I ran a foundation built on empowering women, and yet here I was: unsure, ashamed, and afraid.

The more Derrick drank, the more my confidence wavered. Trust, once effortless, became fragile. I began to question everything. Was he drinking because of me? Did he regret marrying me? Was I enough?

These thoughts consumed me in silence. I'd lie awake at night, staring at the ceiling, wondering if I'd made a mistake. Every time I considered bringing it up, fear stopped me—fear that he'd dismiss me, that I'd push him further away.

So I stayed quiet.

Derrick's drinking became the unspoken elephant in the room, and I threw myself into the renovation as a distraction. We hired a contractor to reimagine the space. I wanted open walls, a modern kitchen—a fresh start. Derrick, ever the pragmatist, pushed back on the costs.

"You know how I feel about spending money unnecessarily," he said during a particularly tense conversation about backsplash tiles.

"And you know how I feel about cutting corners," I snapped.

The tension simmered. I told myself it was just the stress of the renovation.

Still, there were moments of tenderness. Derrick would pull me into his arms unexpectedly, kiss my forehead, and whisper, "I love you. You know that, right?"

And I believed him. But love wasn't enough to quiet the doubts growing in my mind.

I felt like a fraud. I stood on stages telling women to value themselves, to trust their instincts, to never settle. Yet, in my own life, I wasn't following my own advice.

"Am I a hypocrite?" I whispered one night after Derrick had gone to bed.

I didn't have an answer.

The turning point came when Derrick missed a contractor meeting after a night of drinking. I was furious—but more than that, I was hurt.

"Derrick, we need to talk," I said that evening.

"About what?" he asked, defensive.

"This," I said, gesturing around us. "Your drinking, your distance, the way it's affecting us. I can't keep pretending everything's okay."

He sighed, rubbing his temples. "I know I've been drinking more than I should. I just... I don't know how to deal with everything sometimes."

"Then let me help you," I said. "We're a team, Derrick. But I can't do this alone."

It was the first honest conversation we'd had in weeks. It didn't fix everything, but it was a start.

Marriage was harder than I ever imagined. It wasn't just about love—it was about honesty, compromise, and facing the truths neither of us wanted to admit.

As we kept renovating the house and trying to build a life together, I realized I couldn't keep hiding my feelings. If we were going to make it, I had to be honest—with him and with myself.

Because while Derrick was my husband, my partner, my love, I had to remember I was my own rock first.

TAKING THE STEPS TOGETHER

The night Derrick finally admitted he was struggling felt like a breakthrough—a crack in the armor he'd worn for so long. Sitting on the couch, his hands gripping mine, he finally opened up.

"I can't do this on my own," he said, his voice barely above a whisper. "I've been carrying things from my time in the military for years, and I thought I could just push through. But I can't anymore. I need help."

Tears filled my eyes, but I held them back. This wasn't the time for me to break—it was the moment for us to move forward together.

"I'm so proud of you," I said, squeezing his hands. "You don't have to do this alone, Derrick. I'm here every step of the way."

Chapter 10

HEALING TOGETHER

---

*"His journey to healing became ours,
strengthening the love we fought to preserve."*

Derrick returned to counseling, this time focusing on the traumas he'd carried from his time in the military. It wasn't easy for him—a man who prided himself on strength and independence—to admit he needed help again. But he was determined, and that determination reminded me why I fell in love with him in the first place.

We also began couples counseling, creating space to work on our communication and confront the challenges that had built up over the months. Slowly, the walls we'd both put up started to come down.

Through it all, I made sure to remind him that he was loved, valued, and not alone. He didn't have to be perfect; he just had to try. And he did.

With Derrick's renewed commitment to healing and our new home finally complete, life began to feel more stable. The house—once just his—now reflected both of us. The walls were painted in warm, welcoming colors, the kitchen sparkled with the modern touches I'd insisted on, and the living room was filled with photos of our blended families and us.

"This place feels like us," I said one evening as we sat on the back porch, sipping sweet tea and watching the sunset.

"It does," Derrick agreed, wrapping his arm around me. "It feels like home."

Finding our groove as a married couple wasn't easy. We were two independent people, set in our ways, learning to navigate shared spaces and responsibilities. But we were figuring it out, day by day.

Despite the challenges we faced, Derrick's love for me was undeniable. He was a protector, a provider, and a man who believed in taking care of his family. He made me feel safe, cherished, and adored in ways I hadn't felt in years.

Whether it was making sure my car was always filled with gas, cooking breakfast on Sunday mornings, or holding me close during life's storms, Derrick showed his love in the little things. "He loves you," my best friend Latonya said one day over coffee. "I know," I replied with a soft smile. "He really does."

As Derrick continued his journey of healing, I found myself letting go of the fear and doubt that had weighed me down. I stopped hiding my feelings and started trusting in our partnership. We began carving out routines that worked for us—Friday night dinners at our favorite restaurant, lazy Saturday mornings reading the paper together, weekly check-ins where we talked openly about our hopes, fears, and plans for the future, and of course, church on Sundays.

"I think we're finally finding our rhythm," I said one evening as we danced in the living room to our favorite song. "We are," Derrick agreed, his eyes full of love. "And I wouldn't want to do this with anyone else."

LOOKING AHEAD

Life wasn't perfect, but it was ours. Together, we were building something strong, something beautiful, something worth fighting for.

Derrick's commitment to healing wasn't just his journey—it became ours. His counseling sessions were tough, often leaving him emotionally raw, but they opened doors to conversations we'd never had before.

One evening, as we sat in the living room after one of his sessions, he said something that stayed with me.

"Thank you for not giving up on me," Derrick said, his voice heavy with emotion. "I know it hasn't been easy."

"It hasn't," I admitted, placing my hand on his. "But love isn't easy, Derrick. And I love you enough to see this through."

The more Derrick worked on himself, the more I found myself reflecting on my own emotional wounds. I realized that while I'd been strong for him, I also needed to be strong for myself.

PERSONAL GROWTH

I started journaling again—something I hadn't done since before we got married. Writing became my outlet, a way to sort through my feelings, fears, and frustrations. I also joined a support group for spouses of veterans. Hearing other women share their stories made me feel less alone and reminded me that healing is a collective effort, not a solo endeavor.

At one meeting, I shared something I'd kept bottled up. "I've been ashamed to admit that I sometimes feel like I'm not enough for my husband. That his struggles reflect something I'm not doing right," I said, my voice trembling. One of the women, a retired Army wife, leaned over and said, "Honey, his battles aren't yours to fix. You're his partner, not his savior. Just being there is enough."

Those words stayed with me. They gave me the strength to focus on our relationship while also prioritizing my own mental health.

As Derrick made strides in his healing, the change in him was clear. He became more open, more attentive, more present. His laughter returned—so did his sense of humor. We started finding joy in the little things again: cooking dinner together, watching our favorite shows, taking long walks through the neighborhood.

But it wasn't just the good moments that defined our progress— it was the hard conversations, too. The ones where we dug into the roots of our insecurities, fears, and habits.

One night, after a long talk about finances and future plans, Derrick looked at me and said, "I feel like I can finally breathe again. Thank you for being patient with me." I smiled, tears welling up. "We're in this together, Derrick. Always."

Settling into our newly renovated home became a metaphor for our relationship—taking something good and making it even better. We tackled projects side by side, from choosing paint colors to landscaping the yard. Each decision felt like another brick in the foundation of our partnership.

The challenges didn't vanish, but they became manageable. Derrick continued counseling, and I remained his biggest cheerleader. At the same time, I focused on expanding The Color of Pretty foundation, finding purpose and peace in supporting other women.

Derrick and I began planning the next phase of our life—trips we wanted to take, traditions we hoped to start, and dreams we were ready to chase.

"I want us to grow old together," Derrick said one night as we sat on the back porch, stars twinkling above us.

"Me too," I replied, leaning into him. "But only if you keep doing the work."

"I will," he promised, pulling me close.

For the first time in a long time, I believed him. Together, we were stronger. Together, we were unstoppable.

A SEASON OF JOY

Things began to shift in the most beautiful way. Derrick was thriving at work, and I could see how his dedication was finally paying off. When he came home one evening with news of his promotion, the pride on his face made my heart swell.

"They finally recognized what I bring to the table," he said, a grin spreading across his face.

I leapt into his arms. "You deserve this, Derrick. All of it."

The promotion brought a raise, new responsibilities, and— most importantly—a deep sense of fulfillment. Watching him grow professionally while continuing his personal growth was inspiring.

Around the same time, I received an unexpected offer for an exciting new role—a leadership position with another government agency that perfectly aligned with my passions.

When I shared the news with Derrick, he beamed. "That's my wife. Changing lives and chasing dreams."

With both of us thriving professionally, we had more time and energy to focus on each other. For the first time in years, we weren't consumed by raising kids or managing crises. We were empty nesters, and the freedom was exhilarating.

We began traveling together, visiting places we'd always dreamed of. From Martha's Vineyard to the beaches of Jamaica, each trip became a new chapter in our love story.

One evening in Italy, as we sat on a terrace overlooking the Amalfi Coast, Derrick reached for my hand.

"Do you know how much I love you?" he asked, his voice soft but full of conviction.

I smiled, my heart full. "I do. And I hope you know how much I love you, too."

In those moments, the struggles we'd faced felt distant—a testament to the strength we'd built together.

Back home, I was in the final stages of planning the fifth annual *The Color of Pretty* conference. Each year, it grew larger, and this time was no exception. With Derrick's support, I poured my heart into every detail, from selecting speakers to curating impactful workshops.

"I'm so proud of you," Derrick said one night as I reviewed the final agenda. "You've turned your story into a platform that's changing lives."

"And you've been my rock through it all," I replied, leaning over to kiss him.

On the day of the conference, Derrick surprised me by arriving early, dressed sharply in a suit, ready to help with last-minute preparations. As I took the stage to open the event, I spotted him in the front row, his eyes shining with pride.

A NEW CHAPTER TOGETHER

Our days settled into a beautiful rhythm of love, laughter, and purpose. We had found our groove—balancing careers, family, and personal growth in a way that felt intentional and full. There was an ease between us now, a quiet understanding born from weathering storms and choosing each other again and again.

One evening, as we curled up on the couch after dinner with the soft hum of jazz in the background, Derrick turned to me with a look of quiet contentment.

"I feel like we're finally living the life we always dreamed of," he said, his voice warm and steady.

I smiled, resting my head on his shoulder, feeling the calm rise and fall of his breath. "Because we worked for it. Because we fought through the hard parts and never gave up on us."

He kissed my forehead, his touch lingering just long enough to remind me how far we'd come.

Looking ahead, I knew life would still bring its twists and turns, its moments of joy and heartbreak. But for the first time, I wasn't afraid of what was to come. We had built something real—something strong. And whatever the future held, we were ready to face it.

Together.

Chapter 11

THE NIGHT EVERYTHING CHANGED

"The minutes stretched into eternity, each unanswered call a cruel reminder that something was deeply, irreversibly wrong."

---

*L*ife had been smooth—almost too smooth. Derrick and I were in sync, balancing new jobs, therapy sessions, and our shared love of travel. We relished the comfort of our renovated home, savoring small joys like impromptu date nights and lazy Sundays. But life has a way of throwing curveballs, even when everything feels just right.

One evening, everything began to shift. Derrick was on his way home from work, and as usual, we had our routine traffic call—a daily check-in to decompress and reconnect before walking through the front door.

"What's for dinner?" he asked, his voice light.

"Nothing in the fridge," I laughed. "We've officially eaten all the leftovers."

"How about Chinese?"

"Sounds great," I said. "You know my usual—General Tso's chicken, extra broccoli."

"Text it to me," he replied.

I sent my order and made a quick stop at the pharmacy to pick up a prescription. Derrick was grabbing the food and meeting me at home. He was only about five minutes from the restaurant, so I expected him to get there first.

But when I pulled into the driveway about 45 minutes later, his car wasn't there. At first, I didn't think much of it—maybe the restaurant was busy, or he'd stopped to grab something else. But as the minutes passed, a sense of unease began to settle in.

I tried calling him. No answer.

I texted: *Hey babe, everything okay? Let me know when you're on your way.*

Still nothing.

That pit in my stomach—the kind that only forms when something feels deeply, instinctively wrong—began to grow. I paced the living room, glancing out the window every few seconds. It didn't make sense. Derrick never ignored my calls, and he was only minutes from home.

The Chinese food didn't matter anymore. Where was Derrick?

I sat on the couch, phone in hand, running through possible scenarios. Maybe his phone died. Maybe he ran into someone. Maybe traffic was worse than expected. But none of it eased the gnawing fear that something was wrong.

Call after call—no answer. Each ring sent a new wave of panic through me. Each voicemail felt like a door slamming shut. My mind spiraled through a thousand possibilities, none of them good.

By 8:30 PM, I was pacing the living room, gripping my phone so tightly my knuckles turned white. *God, please let him be okay,* I prayed. But as the minutes dragged on, my prayers shifted.

God, this is not your will for my life, I whispered, tears rising. *I can't live like this. I won't. I deserve better.*

I tried calling again—straight to voicemail. I sent another text: *Derrick, I'm worried. Please just let me know you're okay.*

The silence was unbearable.

I had to distract myself—anything to keep my mind from spiraling. I went to the kitchen, grabbed bread, peanut butter, and jelly, and started making a sandwich. My hands shook as I spread the jelly, the knife clinking against the plate. I wasn't even hungry, but I needed to *do* something—anything—to keep from falling apart.

By 9 PM, worry had turned into something darker: fear, anger, helplessness. Four hours had passed since I'd last heard his voice. Four hours of unanswered calls and texts. Four hours of imagining the worst.

Do I call his parents? The kids? His brother?

I stared at my phone, torn. I didn't want to alarm anyone if there was nothing to worry about—but what if there was?

Who can I confide in? The truth was, I felt completely alone. Ashamed. Embarrassed. I didn't want to admit I had no idea where my husband was, that I was sitting here terrified, with no answers.

I leaned against the counter, gripping the edge so hard it hurt. Tears spilled over, and I let them fall. *Why is this happening again?* I thought.

Midnight. The silence in the house was suffocating. The ticking clock felt deafening, each second stretching longer without Derrick. I sat curled on the couch, phone in my lap, staring at the screen. Call after call had gone unanswered. Each voicemail was more frantic than the last.

Where is he? The question looped through my mind like a broken record.

The pit in my stomach had grown into a cavernous ache. I thought about calling his parents or brother, but what would I even say? *Hey, Derrick isn't home, and I think he's been drinking again.* The thought made me feel small. Ashamed.

I tried to distract myself, flipping through TV channels, but nothing held my attention. My mind raced, each possibility darker than the last.

What if he got into an accident? What if he's in trouble and can't reach me? Or worse—what if he chose not to come home?

I stood and began pacing, anxiety bubbling over me. "God, this is not your will for my life," I whispered, my voice shaking. "I can't live like this. I won't."

I stopped pacing and grabbed my phone again, scrolling through my contacts, debating who to call. But the truth was, I felt completely alone.

I run a foundation for women, I thought bitterly. *I help them find strength and their voice. And here I am, afraid to admit the cracks in my own life.*

I finally sat back down, wrapping a blanket around myself like armor against the growing fear. My eyes landed on the wedding photo on the mantle—Derrick smiling proudly, me beaming in my white dress. We looked so happy. So full of hope.

"Where are you, Derrick?" I whispered into the empty room. Frustration and hurt pressed heavy on my chest. By 2 a.m., the silence was unbearable. My anger and disappointment warred with exhaustion until I drifted into a restless sleep, still clutching my phone.

When I jolted awake, the clock read 5 a.m. The ache of worry hadn't faded. If anything, it had deepened. I remembered I had to be in the office—it was Friday, and while I usually worked from home, there was a meeting I couldn't miss.

The routine of showering and dressing offered little comfort. I moved on autopilot, my mind racing. I called Derrick's phone three more times—each met with the same hollow voicemail. Every unanswered call deepened my frustration and fear.

Standing in front of the mirror, brushing my hair, I stared at my reflection. My eyes were red and puffy from crying, a tight knot forming in my stomach. "Do I call his mother?" I murmured. Derrick was a momma's boy—he often confided in her about things he couldn't share with anyone else.

But the thought of calling her made me hesitate. What would I even say? That my husband hadn't come home, and I had no idea where he was? That I was scared something had happened—or worse, that he was drinking again?

I grabbed my bag and keys, forcing myself to focus on the day ahead. Just as I reached the door, I tried his phone one last time.

It rang. My heart leapt—then sank as it went to voicemail.

I gripped the steering wheel tightly on the drive to work, my thoughts bouncing between anger and worry. *Where could he be? Why hasn't he called?*

AT THE OFFICE

By the time I got to the office, I was running on autopilot. I greeted my coworkers with a forced smile, trying to mask the turmoil churning inside me. My phone sat on the desk, dark and lifeless, mocking my anxiety.

I made it through the morning meeting, though I could barely recall what was said. My mind kept drifting to Derrick, replaying every possible scenario.

By 10 a.m., the gnawing fear had taken over. Derrick had never done anything like this before—no calls, no texts, no explanation. The anger I'd clung to all night was now eclipsed by pure, relentless worry.

I called his phone again and again, each ring stretching like an eternity. Then suddenly, someone answered. Relief hit me—then vanished when I heard an unfamiliar voice.

"Hello?" a man said, his tone firm and unfamiliar.

"Who is this?" I asked, my voice shaking.

"Who's this?" he replied, matching my urgency.

"This is Lola, Derrick's wife. Who are you?" My panic spiked with each word.

"This is Howard County Police," he said, and my heart dropped.

"What? Howard County Police?" My voice cracked. "What's going on? What happened to Derrick? Is he okay?"

There was a pause. "Ma'am, can you confirm your husband's name?"

"It's Derrick Thompson," I said quickly, hands trembling. "Please, what's wrong? Is he hurt? Is he okay?"

Another pause. Then, "I'm writing your number down, but the phone is about to die. I'll call you right back."

"No!" I cried, voice breaking. "Don't hang up! What's wrong with my husband? Please, just tell me!"

But the line went dead.

I stood frozen in the middle of my office, the silence crushing. My mind raced. Was he in an accident? In the hospital? I began pacing, clutching my phone like it was the only thing tethering me to reality.

"God, please," I whispered, tears slipping down my cheeks. "Don't let this be the worst."

Minutes stretched into what felt like hours. I called his phone again—straight to voicemail. My thoughts spiraled. I considered calling his mother or brother but couldn't bring myself to do it. What if I panicked them for no reason?

I sat at my desk, heart pounding, the officer's words looping through my mind: *Howard County Police. The phone is about to die. I'll call you right back.*

Every second stretched endlessly. Five minutes. Ten. Fifteen. Still nothing.

I tried to focus on work, fingers hovering over the keyboard, but I couldn't type a single coherent sentence. The worry pressed against my chest, just beneath the surface, ready to spill over. I glanced around at my coworkers, all moving through their day like everything was normal.

Stay neutral, Lola. Hold it together.

But how could I? My husband was missing—or worse—and I didn't even know where to begin.

Finally, I grabbed my phone, hands trembling. There was only one person I could call—Latonya. She was my anchor. The one person who wouldn't judge me or downplay what I was feeling.

I stepped into an empty conference room and dialed.

"Hey, girl," Latonya answered, cheerful as always. "What's up?"

The sound of her voice broke me. I didn't even realize I was crying until I tried to speak—and the words came out fractured.

"Latonya," I managed, voice shaking. "I need help. I don't know what to do."

"Lola? What's wrong?" Her tone shifted instantly, laced with concern.

"It's Derrick," I said, panic rising. "He didn't come home last night. I've been calling and calling, and this morning, someone finally answered—but it wasn't him. It was a police officer. He said Derrick was involved in something, but the phone died before he could tell me what."

"Oh my God," Latonya murmured. "Did they call you back?"

"No," I whispered, shaking my head though she couldn't see me. "I've been sitting here waiting. I don't know where he is or what's happening. I'm at work, but I can't think, I can't— I'm scared, Latonya. What if it's serious? What if—"

"Lola," she cut in gently but firmly. "Breathe. I need you to take a deep breath, okay? You can't think clearly if you're panicked. We'll take this one step at a time."

I closed my eyes and inhaled deeply, then exhaled, trying to steady myself.

"Okay," I whispered.

"Now," Latonya said, calm but focused, "did they give you any information at all? A name, a number, where he is?"

"No," I said, my voice trembling. "Nothing concrete. The officer just said he'd call me back, but the phone died before I got any details."

Latonya let out a thoughtful hum. "Okay, here's what you're going to do. Call 911 or 311 and explain everything. They should be able to tell you if Derrick is in custody or give you some information."

"Okay," I said, feeling a flicker of clarity amid the chaos. "That's a good idea."

"I'll keep my phone close," Latonya said. "Call me as soon as you know anything."

I nodded, even though she couldn't see me. "I will."

"Lola," she said gently, "take a breath. You've been carrying this all morning, and it's too heavy. Let's say a quick prayer together before you make that call."

Tears stung my eyes as I swallowed the lump in my throat. "Okay," I whispered.

"Father God," Latonya began, her voice steady and full of faith. "We come to You asking for peace, clarity, and protection. Lord, cover Derrick wherever he is. Bring him home safely. Strengthen Lola—remind her she's not alone. Guide her through this moment. In Jesus' name, Amen."

"Amen," I whispered, a wave of calm settling over me.

"You've got this," Latonya said. "Call me back when you hear something."

"Thank you," I said, my voice barely audible.

After hanging up, I stared at my phone, trying to find the courage to make the next call. Finally, with a deep breath, I dialed 911, my fingers trembling with each press. The line connected, and a calm voice answered.

"911, what's your emergency?"

I gripped the phone tighter. "Hi, my name is Lola, and I think my husband might be in custody. I got a call earlier from the Howard County Police, but the phone died before they could explain. I don't know what's going on, and I need help."

The operator's voice remained calm and professional. "Okay, ma'am, let me gather some information. What is your husband's name?"

I gave her Derrick's full name, my voice shaking with each word.

"Thank you," she said. "I'm going to check our records to see if we have any information on him. Please hold."

As the line went silent, I closed my eyes and gripped the edge of the desk. Each second felt like an eternity as I waited for her to return with an answer.

The officer's vague advice to "be calm" only made things worse. My mind raced through every possible scenario, each darker than the last. How could they tell me to stay calm when they had no answers? I paced back and forth in my office, clutching my phone. Minutes dragged on like hours, and every second of silence felt like a weight on my chest.

I tried to focus on breathing, as Latonya had said, but the panic was overwhelming. Just when I thought I couldn't take it anymore, my phone rang. I snatched it up so quickly that I nearly dropped it.

"This is Lola," I said, my voice trembling.

"Mrs. Thompson, this is Officer Reynolds," the voice said, slightly hesitant. "We've been able to piece together more details, and I'm calling to update you."

His line of questioning tested every ounce of my patience. "What's his full name? Address? Any medical conditions?" he asked, his tone methodical.

I could barely contain my frustration. "I've already told you everything I know! Why are you asking me these questions without telling me anything? What's going on with Derrick?" My voice was sharper than I intended, but the stress was too much.

"Mrs. Thompson," the officer said firmly, "I need you to calm down. I want to come to where you are so we can discuss this properly."

"No, you will not," I snapped. "I'm at work, and I cannot have this kind of conversation here."

"Mrs. Thompson, please," he said, his voice softening. "It's important that we talk in person. I understand this is difficult, but I need to explain the situation fully."

I hesitated, torn between the need to know and the fear of what he might say. My chest tightened, and my hands trembled as I tried to stay composed.

Finally, I sighed. "Fine. I'll leave work and meet you at the house. Can you meet me there?"

"Yes, ma'am," he said, his tone steady but sympathetic. "I'll head there now. Take your time, and please drive safely."

I hung up and sat at my desk, my heart racing. The weight of the unknown was unbearable. I grabbed my purse and laptop, muttering something to my supervisor about a personal emergency. My coworkers barely looked up, but I could feel the panic rising as I walked out.

As I drove home, every possible scenario raced through my mind. Was Derrick hurt? Was he in trouble? Or was this another consequence of the drinking we thought we'd left behind? The questions swirled, and by the time I pulled into the driveway, the officer's car was already there, waiting.

Taking a deep breath, I stepped out, bracing myself for whatever news was about to come.

Latonya parked behind me, worry etched on her face as she stepped out and met me by the driveway. Without a word, she took my hand—a silent gesture of support. Together, we walked toward the house, my feet feeling like lead. Time seemed to slow, every second stretching endlessly.

"Why did he tell you to go home?" Latonya asked, her voice hushed and filled with concern.

"I don't know," I replied, shaking my head. My heart pounded so hard it felt like it might burst. "He wouldn't tell me anything. Just said he needed to talk to me in person."

Latonya squeezed my hand as we reached the front door. I fumbled with my keys, my hands trembling so badly it took three tries to fit the key in the lock. Finally, the door swung open, and the officer stood in the entryway, his expression grim.

"Ms. Thompson, thank you for coming home," he said gently, stepping back to let us inside. The house felt cold, heavy with the weight of the unknown. Latonya stayed close, her presence the only thing keeping me from collapsing under the pressure of my racing thoughts.

"Officer," I began, my voice shaky but firm. "What's going on? Why did you make me come here? Please, just tell me."

He took a deep breath, sorrow in his eyes. "Ms. Thompson," he said, his tone low and measured, "there's no easy way to say this, and I wanted to make sure you were in a safe space before I told you. Your husband, Derrick, experienced a cardiac arrest earlier this evening. Despite the best efforts of the paramedics, he… he didn't make it."

The words hit like a freight train. My knees buckled, and Latonya caught me before I hit the floor.

"No," I gasped, shaking my head violently. "No, no, no! That's not true! He was fine! He was just picking up dinner last night!"

"I'm so sorry," the officer said, his voice heavy with compassion. "Your husband was found unresponsive at a hotel on South Avenue. Staff called 911 when they noticed something was wrong. The paramedics did everything they could, but… he didn't make it."

The words didn't register at first. A hotel? My mind struggled to connect the dots. Derrick was supposed to be picking up dinner. Why was he at a hotel? My body stiffened as a fresh wave of panic bubbled up.

"A hotel?" I echoed, my voice barely above a whisper, as if saying it out loud would make it real. "What was he doing there?"

The officer hesitated, his face sympathetic but guarded. "I don't have all the details, Mrs. Thompson. I can only tell you that he was found alone, and there was no sign of foul play."

My mind raced. Alone? Why was he there? Why hadn't he come home? Questions flooded my thoughts, each one sharper and more painful than the last. Latonya's hand tightened on mine, grounding me as my heart threatened to splinter into a thousand pieces.

"Lola," Latonya said softly, her voice steady. "Breathe. We'll figure this out. One step at a time."

I nodded numbly, but my thoughts were spiraling. Had Derrick been hiding something from me? Was this why he hadn't come home? Guilt crept in at the edges of my grief. I should've done more. I should've known something was wrong.

"Do you know… why he was there?" I asked the officer, my voice trembling with a mixture of pain and dread.

The officer shook his head. "I'm afraid I don't have that information. We're still looking into the circumstances. For now, I suggest focusing on taking care of yourself. This is a lot to process."

A hotel. Alone. Gone. The words echoed in my mind like a cruel refrain. Derrick was gone.

"No!" I screamed, tears streaming down my face. "He was just supposed to pick up dinner! He was fine! He was fine this morning!" My voice cracked as the weight of the words settled into my chest. Latonya pulled me into her arms, whispering words of comfort, though I could barely hear her over the sound of my own sobs.

"This can't be happening," I whispered, my voice trembling. "He can't be gone. He just… he just can't."

The officer gave me a moment, then gently added, "If there's anyone else you'd like us to contact, we're here to help. And if you need any support, please don't hesitate to reach out."

I could barely nod. My mind was spinning, racing through every memory, every moment, every conversation I'd ever had with Derrick. The last text I sent him—my usual order for dinner—flashed through my mind.

After what felt like an eternity, the officer finally stood, his face still carrying that mix of compassion and discomfort. "Mrs. Thompson, I know this is overwhelming. I'm leaving you with the contact information for the medical examiner's office. They'll be able to give you the official cause of death once their report is completed. I'm so sorry for your loss."

I nodded mechanically as he handed me a card, my hands trembling as I took it. Latonya stepped in, her presence steady and reassuring.

"Thank you, Officer," she said on my behalf, guiding him to the door as I stood frozen in the living room, staring at the small piece of cardstock with the medical examiner's information printed neatly on it.

Chapter 12

A LIFE SHATTERED IN SECONDS

"I held the phone in my trembling hands, searching for answers in the emptiness left behind."

The door closed behind the officer, and the silence in the house was deafening. My mind was a whirlwind of emotions—grief, confusion, anger, and disbelief. I felt like I was floating, detached from my own body.

"Lola," Latonya said gently, breaking through my haze. "Sit down, honey. Just for a minute."

I let her guide me to the couch, my legs barely able to hold me. The card was still clutched in my hand, my eyes fixed on it like it held all the answers. "The medical examiner…" I started, my voice weak and unsteady. "I have to call. I have to know what happened."

"And you will," Latonya said, sitting beside me and placing a hand on my back. "But not right this second. You've been through so much in the last few hours. Let's take a moment to breathe."

Breathe. Such a simple instruction, but it felt impossible. How was I supposed to breathe when the man I loved—the man I had built a life with—was gone?

I felt tears burn in my eyes, and they spilled over before I could stop them. "Why, Latonya?" I whispered, my voice cracking. "Why was he there? What was he doing? I don't understand…"

She pulled me into a hug, letting me cry into her shoulder. "I don't know, Lola," she said softly. "But we'll get through this. We'll figure it out together. You're not alone."

Her words were a lifeline, but they couldn't quiet the storm raging inside me. Deep down, I knew this was only the beginning of a long, painful journey. There were too many questions and not enough answers. But for now, all I could do was sit there, holding the card and hoping it would bring the clarity I so desperately needed.

Latonya stayed by my side, her calm presence grounding me as I struggled to process what had just happened. After a few minutes of silence, she gently asked, "Do you want me to make the call for you? To the medical examiner's office?"

I shook my head, wiping the tears from my face. "No, I have to do it. I need to hear it for myself." My voice was shaky, but there was a determination in it that surprised even me.

Latonya nodded, handing me her phone. "Okay, but I'll be right here."

I dialed the number on the card with trembling fingers, each ring stretching into eternity. Finally, a woman answered, her tone professional but kind. "Howard County Medical Examiner's Office, how can I help you?"

"This is Lola Thompson," I said, my voice barely above a whisper. "My husband, Derrick Thompson, passed away, and the police told me to call for more information."

There was a pause on the other end. "I'm so sorry for your loss, Mrs. Thompson. Let me pull up his file. One moment, please."

The hold music felt surreal, almost mocking in its upbeat melody. I gripped Latonya's hand, drawing strength from her presence. When the woman returned, her voice was softer. "Mrs. Thompson, I can confirm that your husband, Derrick Thompson, was brought to us earlier today. The preliminary report indicates that he suffered a cardiac arrest."

"A cardiac arrest?" I repeated, my mind racing. "Was it... was it natural? Was there anything else?"

"There's no indication of foul play," she said carefully. "However, the toxicology results are still pending. Those usually take a few weeks. Once the full report is completed, we'll contact you with the details."

"Thank you," I said, though the words felt hollow. I hung up and stared at the phone in my hand. A cardiac arrest. No foul play. Toxicology pending. What did it all mean? And why was he at a hotel?

Latonya gently squeezed my hand. "What did they say?"

I repeated the conversation, my voice flat. "Cardiac arrest. No foul play. Toxicology results pending."

She nodded, brow furrowed. "Okay, that's a start. But, Lola, I know what you're thinking. Don't go down that rabbit hole yet. Let's wait for the full report."

"But why was he at that hotel?" I asked, my voice breaking. "He told me he was picking up dinner. None of this makes sense."

"I know," she said softly. "And we'll figure it out. But right now, you need to take it one step at a time. Let's focus on getting through today."

I nodded, though the weight of my questions was crushing. "I don't know if I can do this," I whispered.

"You can," Latonya said firmly. "You're one of the strongest women I know, Lola. And you don't have to do it alone. You've got me, the girls, your family. We'll get through this together."

Her words steadied me, but the ache in my chest didn't ease. I looked around the house Derrick and I had worked so hard to make a home, and it felt unbearably empty.

"I just don't understand," I whispered, more to myself than to her. "How did this happen? Why did this happen?"

Latonya didn't have an answer, and neither did I. But as the hours passed, one thing was clear: my life would never be the same.

She gently placed her hands on my shoulders, her voice calm but resolute. "Lola, we need to let Derrick's family know. His parents, his girls, his brother—they deserve to hear it from you. And you should call your mom and Mikaela too. You don't have to do this alone."

I nodded slowly as if moving through the fog. My mind was spinning, my body numb. "I don't even know what to say," I admitted, tears welling in my eyes again. "How do I tell them this? How do I say he's gone?"

Latonya pulled out her phone and started dialing. "I'll help you. Let's start with your mom and Mikaela. They'll be here for you. We'll figure out the rest together."

I stared at my phone, hesitating, then pulled up my mom's contact. My thumb hovered over the call button for what felt like forever. Finally, I pressed it and held the phone to my ear.

"Hi, baby," my mom answered, her voice warm and familiar.

The sound of her voice broke something in me. I burst into tears, unable to speak. "Mom," I sobbed. "It's Derrick... he's gone. He's gone, Mom."

There was a sharp intake of breath. "Oh my God, Lola. What happened? Are you okay? Where are you?"

"I'm at home," I managed through my tears. "The police said it was cardiac arrest. I don't know, Mom. I don't know what's happening."

"I'm coming over right now," she said, her voice trembling. "Don't move. I'll be there soon."

I hung up, hands shaking, and looked at Latonya. She gave me a small, encouraging nod. "One step at a time," she said.

Next was Mikaela. My hands trembled even more as I dialed. When she answered, her cheerful voice felt like a cruel contrast to the weight in my chest.

"Hey, Mom! What's up?"

Her carefree tone made me hesitate. How could I shatter her world like this? "Mikaela," I began, my voice breaking. "Sweetheart, something's happened. Derrick... he passed away."

Silence. Then a shaky, "What? Mom, what are you talking about? What happened?"

I explained as best I could, each word a dagger. By the time I hung up, I was drained. Mikaela said she'd catch the next flight home.

Latonya touched my arm gently. "You're doing great, Lola. Now, we need to call Derrick's parents. Do you want me to make the call?"

I shook my head, my voice trembling. "No, I think I should call his brother, Vern. He'll know how to talk to their parents. I can't make that call… and he'll know how to tell the girls, too."

Latonya nodded, her expression soft. "That's a good idea, Lola. Let's call Vern. He'll know how to handle it."

I scrolled through my phone and found Vern's number, my hand shaking as I pressed call. He picked up after a few rings, his voice upbeat and unsuspecting.

"Hey, Lola! What's up?"

His familiar tone made my chest tighten. I took a shaky breath, my voice barely above a whisper. "Vern… something's happened. It's Derrick."

There was a pause, and then his voice turned serious. "What do you mean? What's going on?"

I couldn't hold back the tears. "He's gone, Vern. Derrick's gone. The police said it was cardiac arrest. I—I don't know what to do."

Silence. Then, a deep, broken sigh. "Oh my God," Vern said. "I can't believe this. Where are you? Are you okay?"

"I'm at home," I said, wiping my face. "The officer came here to tell me. I just… I can't call your parents or the girls. I need you, Vern. Please."

"You did the right thing calling me," he said firmly, though emotion crept into his voice. "I'll take care of it. I'll call Mom and Dad, and I'll talk to the girls. Don't worry about that."

"Thank you," I whispered, grief and relief tangling in my chest.

"I'm coming over," Vern added. "I'll be there as soon as I can. Just sit tight, Lola. You're not alone in this."

When the call ended, I let out a shaky breath. Latonya placed a comforting hand on my back.

"You made the right call, Lola. Vern will handle it. And we'll all be here for you."

I nodded, though the weight of it all still felt crushing. At least now, I wasn't carrying it alone.

Latonya looked at me with a firm, gentle expression. "Lola, you need to call Audra. You know she'll be here in a heartbeat. That's just who she is—she'll drop everything. Right now, you need your whole circle around you."

I nodded again, my throat too tight to speak. Latonya handed me my phone. My hands trembled as I scrolled to Audra's number. I hesitated, staring at her name. Latonya gave me a soft nudge.

"It's okay," she whispered. "She'll want to be here for you."

I hit the call button. After just one ring, Audra picked up.

"Hey, girl!" she said cheerfully. "What's up?"

Her upbeat tone shattered me. I choked on a sob. "Audra," I managed through the tears.

Her voice changed instantly. "Lola? What's wrong? What happened?"

"It's Derrick…" I paused, searching for the words. "He's gone."

Stunned silence followed, then a sharp intake of breath. "Oh my God. Lola, I'm coming right now. Are you at home?"

"Yes," I whispered. "I'm home."

"Don't move. I'll be there in 15 minutes." Her voice was steady, but the urgency was unmistakable.

I hung up and let the phone drop into my lap. Latonya sat beside me, wrapping an arm around my shoulders.

"See? She's already on her way. You're not alone, Lola. We're all here for you."

I nodded numbly, leaning into her. The room felt unbearably quiet, even with her beside me. My mind was a storm—grief, shock, disbelief. I couldn't begin to process it.

Fifteen minutes felt endless, but true to her word, Audra arrived in record time. She burst through the door, face pale with worry, and crossed the room to pull me into a tight hug.

"Oh, Lola," she murmured, voice breaking. "I'm so sorry. I'm so, so sorry."

Her presence was a sliver of comfort—a light cutting through the dark. For the first time since this nightmare began, I felt like I could breathe, even if just barely. My circle was forming around me, and though I couldn't imagine getting through this, I knew I didn't have to do it alone.

Audra pulled back slightly, her hands still on my shoulders, eyes searching mine. "Lola, have you eaten? What can we do for you right now?"

I shook my head, realizing I hadn't eaten since the night before. My stomach turned at the thought, but I knew I had to take care of myself—if not for me, then for the people holding me up.

"I'm not hungry," I whispered. "I don't even know what I need."

Latonya stepped in, her voice firm but gentle. "You need to stay strong. You don't have to eat much, but a little something will help. I'll make tea and toast, okay? Just stay here with Audra."

Before I could respond, she was already heading to the kitchen. Audra guided me back to the couch, her arm still around me.

"You don't need all the answers right now," she said softly. "Just take it one breath at a time. We're here, and we're not going anywhere."

Tears welled up again—grief mixed with gratitude.

"Thank you," I said, my voice cracking. "I don't know what I'd do without you both."

"You'll never have to find out," Audra replied. "We're your family, Lola. We've got you."

Latonya returned a few moments later, setting a tray with tea and buttered toast on the coffee table. "Here you go," she said, settling beside me again. "Just a few bites, okay? And sip the tea— it'll calm your nerves."

I reached for the mug, its warmth grounding me. A small sip of chamomile soothed the tightness in my chest. With their quiet encouragement, I managed a few bites of toast—each one an effort, but a step forward.

Sitting there with my friends, a flicker of strength stirred within me. I didn't know how I'd face the days ahead, but at least I wouldn't be facing them alone.

Audra and Latonya exchanged a glance, silently aligned. Audra picked up her phone and stepped into the hallway, her voice low and steady as she began making calls. Latonya stayed close, scrolling through her contacts.

"I'll start with Karen and Shelly," she said softly, sitting beside me. "They'll want to know what's going on. They'll want to be here."

I nodded slightly, still clutching the warm mug. My mind was blank, my body disconnected. Grief pressed hard against my chest, making it difficult to breathe.

Audra's voice floated in from the hallway, calm and composed as she relayed the news. Latonya dialed Karen, her tone gentle but firm. "We're at Lola's house now," she said. "She needs us."

As they made call after call, I sat motionless, staring at the untouched toast. The words they spoke felt distant as if they belonged to someone else's life. Derrick was gone, and I couldn't grasp what that meant.

Audra returned, her expression soft but resolute. "Everyone's on their way," she said, sitting on my other side. "We've got you, Lola. You don't have to do anything right now. Let us take care of it."

Latonya set her phone down and took my hand. "It's okay to feel lost," she said gently. "We'll help you through this, step by step."

I swallowed hard, my throat tight with unshed tears. "I don't even know what to do next," I whispered.

"You don't have to know," Audra said. "Just breathe. Lean on us. We'll figure it out together."

And in that moment, surrounded by the steady presence of my friends, I realized that even in my darkest hour, I wasn't alone.

Latonya nodded solemnly, her hand still resting on mine. "Of course, Lola. Derrick was an incredible man, and that's what people need to remember—not the struggles, not the pain, just the love, strength, and devotion he gave to everyone around him."

I swallowed hard, the lump in my throat refusing to ease. "He had his demons, but don't we all?" I said softly, my voice trembling. "He loved me. He loved his family. That's what matters."

Latonya and I agreed—no one else would know about the drinking. I couldn't bear the questions or the judgment. I wanted Derrick to be remembered for the man he truly was.

Latonya squeezed my hand. "That's exactly what matters. And you don't owe anyone an explanation. People will grieve in their own way, but we'll keep his memory pure and dignified."

I nodded, grateful for her understanding. "I just can't face the questions, the sideways looks. People think they know everything about someone's life, but they don't. They didn't see how hard he worked, how much he cared."

"They didn't see the way he looked at you," Latonya added. "Or how he always made sure everyone around him was taken care of. That's what they need to remember, and we'll make sure they do."

Tears welled up again as I looked at her. "Thank you, Latonya. For everything."

She smiled gently. "That's what sisters are for. You're not in this alone, Lola. We'll honor him the way he deserves—together."

As we sat there, a small but steady resolve began to rise within me. Derrick's story wouldn't be defined by his struggles. I would make sure his legacy was one of love, strength, and all the good he brought into the world. That's what he deserved. That's what I would give him.

Chapter 13

SAYING GOODBYE TOO SOON

"How do you plan a farewell for someone who was supposed to be your forever?"

Only a day had passed, yet it felt like time had frozen. Just yesterday, we were together—now, families from near and far had gathered, each person absorbing the news in their own way. When they heard about Derrick, disbelief washed over their faces, a mix of shock and the weight of grief.

The sorrow was heavy, settling over us like an unspoken truth we weren't ready to confront. But amid the pain, there was so much love. My family surrounded me, holding me up when I felt like falling apart, offering support in ways I never knew I needed.

We had been married only six months after three years together. It wasn't enough time. It would never be enough.

As the days unfolded, so did the reality of my loss. The house felt emptier and quieter, as if it, too, mourned Derrick's absence. Every corner held a memory—his laughter in the kitchen as he tried (and failed) to perfect my mother's sweet potato pie, the way he hummed while reading on the couch, the scent of his cologne still clinging to the pillows.

Family stayed close, filling the space with warmth, stories, and quiet reminders that I wasn't alone. My mother fussed over me, ensuring I ate, while my aunts moved between prayer and fond memories of Derrick's charm. My cousins, always the lighthearted ones, did their best to stir laughter into the air, reminding me that joy still had a place, even in sorrow.

But the nights were the hardest. When the house fell silent and loneliness pressed against my chest, I found myself reaching for him in the dark, only to meet empty sheets. Sleep slipped away, grief settling in like an uninvited guest—relentless, unyielding.

One evening, Latonya sat beside me on the couch, her presence steady and familiar. She didn't say much—she didn't have to. She simply held my hand, a quiet promise that she wasn't going anywhere.

"You're stronger than you think," she finally whispered.

I wasn't sure I believed her, but I held onto her words anyway. Because in that moment, when my world felt shattered, I needed to believe strength would find me again.

PLANNING

With the weekend behind me, Monday arrived with a weight heavier than I had ever known. Everywhere I turned, someone was asking, "Are you ready to begin planning the homegoing services?" The very thought made my stomach turn. How could I plan to say goodbye to the man I had planned to spend forever with?

Just then, my phone rang. It was Benita from our church. Her voice was soft yet steady, filled with the kind of warmth that only comes from someone who has walked this road before.

"Lola, I know this is hard," she said gently. "But you don't have to do it alone. Let's take it one step at a time. Why don't you come up to the church? We'll go over everything together."

I hesitated, but I knew I couldn't put it off forever. "Okay," I whispered.

Mikaela, ever my rock, insisted on going with me. "You don't have to do this alone, Mom," she reminded me as she squeezed my hand.

Meanwhile, I asked Derrick's parents and children to assist with the funeral home arrangements. I wanted them to have a say in every detail, to feel included in honoring his life. This wasn't just my loss—it was ours.

Planning a funeral for my husband of only six months... how was I supposed to do this? We had just started to find our rhythm as a couple—blending our lives, working through challenges, and, I thought, overcoming Derrick's demons. And now, just like that, I was left to figure out how to say goodbye.

Benita was a godsend. She walked me through every painful decision—from the worship songs to the order of service, even down to the choreography of the procession. Her presence was steady, her guidance unwavering. "You don't have to carry this alone, Lola," she reminded me more than once.

But no amount of planning could have prepared me for the actual day.

The morning of the funeral was the hardest moment of my life. My heart felt like it was being crushed under the weight of grief. I prayed. I cried. Then I prayed again. None of it made sense.

How do you go from having dinner with someone one week to planning their funeral the next? How do you reconcile the laughter, the love, the shared dreams, only to be left with an empty space where they used to be?

As I walked into the church, the reality hit me like a wave I couldn't outrun. The sanctuary was packed—family, friends, colleagues, people whose lives Derrick had touched in ways I hadn't known. Faces were somber, eyes heavy with sorrow. I heard the hushed whispers and saw the silent tears.

And yet, as I took my seat at the front, I knew I had to be strong—not just for myself, but for Mikaela, for Derrick's children, and for his parents. I closed my eyes, took a deep breath, and whispered the only words I could find:

"God, carry me through this."

As the service began, the choir's voices filled the sanctuary, wrapping me in a familiar comfort I didn't know I needed. The music swelled, every lyric feeling like it was written for this exact moment—painful yet healing, sorrowful yet full of faith.

Derrick's parents sat beside me, their hands clasped tightly together. His children were there, their faces a mixture of grief and quiet strength. Mikaela held my hand—a silent source of support as if she knew I needed the touch of someone who loved me unconditionally.

One by one, people stood to share their memories of Derrick. His best friend spoke of his laughter, his resilience, how he made even the hardest days bearable. His coworkers talked about his passion, his generosity, and how he lifted others even while carrying his own burdens.

Then it was my turn.

I hadn't prepared a speech—I didn't know how to put my love, my pain, and my memories into words. But as I stood at the podium, looking out at the faces gathered to honor him, I spoke from my heart.

"Derrick wasn't perfect, but he was good. He loved deeply, cared fiercely, and never stopped trying to be better. Our time together was too short, but I thank God for every moment—for the love, the laughter, the lessons. Derrick, you were loved. You are loved. And you will never be forgotten."

A hush fell over the room. Then, soft murmurs of agreement, sniffles, and nods.

As the casket was slowly carried out, I felt the weight of finality settle on my chest. This was it—the end of our time together on this earth. But even in the pain, I knew it wasn't the end of his story. His life, his love, his struggles and triumphs lived on in everyone who loved him.

And somehow, through the grief, I knew I would carry him with me. Always.

FINDING MY WAY THROUGH THE GRIEF

In the days following the funeral, the world around me felt like a blur. People came and went, offering condolences, dropping off food I barely touched, reminding me to take care of myself. But how do you take care of yourself when a part of you is missing?

Nights were the hardest. The silence of the house was deafening without Derrick—no late-night conversations, no sound of his laughter, no warmth beside me. I would lie awake, staring at the ceiling, asking God the same question over and over: Why?

Mikaela stayed with me for a few weeks, grounding me in a way I hadn't realized I needed. She kept me busy—getting me up to eat, encouraging walks, reminding me of the life I still had to live.

One evening, as we sat on the couch watching one of Derrick's favorite shows, she turned to me and said, "Mom, you're going to be okay."

I wanted to believe her, but I wasn't sure how.

Then, one morning, I woke up and realized I hadn't cried myself to sleep the night before. A small victory—but a victory, nonetheless. I knew I couldn't stay in this place of sadness forever. Derrick wouldn't have wanted that.

I turned to my faith, leaning into God's presence in ways I never had before. I prayed harder, listened more closely, and sought comfort in scripture. I began journaling again, pouring my emotions onto the page, allowing the pain to exist without letting it consume me.

One day, I received a message from a woman who had attended The Color of Pretty conference. She had just lost her husband unexpectedly and was struggling to find her way through the grief.

"I don't know how to do this," she wrote. "I feel lost."

I knew that feeling all too well.

I called her, and for the first time in weeks, I felt purpose stir in me. I shared my story, my pain, my struggles—and somehow, through my words, gave her a little hope.

That conversation lit a spark.

What if my pain wasn't just mine to carry? What if I could use it to help others walking the same path?

From that moment on, I made a choice. I would honor Derrick not by drowning in grief but by living. By helping. By continuing to build The Color of Pretty into a space for women navigating life's hardest moments.

I launched a new initiative—*Beauty From Ashes*—a support program for women experiencing grief and loss. We gathered in small groups, shared our stories, and leaned on each other in ways only those who had been through it could understand.

The first meeting was intimate: five of us, sitting in a circle, tears flowing, hearts open. But over time, the circle grew. More women came, seeking solace, finding strength, learning to rebuild.

Derrick's death had broken me—but it had also given me a new mission.

I wasn't just surviving. I was transforming.

And for the first time since losing him, I knew—deep in my soul—I was going to be okay.

A NEW BEGINNING

The new initiative was off to a strong start, and after about a month, I finally returned to work. Each day felt like a delicate balancing act—showing up for others while still trying to find my own footing. But no matter how busy I kept myself, I couldn't escape the weight of Derrick's absence. His presence lingered in every corner of the house—the scent of his cologne on his favorite chair, his shoes by the door, and the echo of his laughter in my memory.

Each morning, I woke up in a space that felt both familiar and foreign, comforting and suffocating. I knew I couldn't stay. As much as I wanted to hold on to the memories, the walls of this house held too much pain.

I began weighing my options—reaching out to investors, exploring new possibilities—but the longer I stayed, the clearer it became: I needed a fresh start. Remaining here would only keep me tethered to the past.

One evening, after much prayer and soul-searching, I picked up the phone and called Nora, my longtime realtor. When she answered, I could hear the surprise in her voice.

"Lola? Oh my goodness, I was just thinking about you," she said warmly.

I took a deep breath. "Nora, I need to sell the house."

Silence.

She knew what this house meant. She had helped Derrick and me sell my townhome not long ago. We had chosen this place together—imagined a future here. And now, that future was gone.

"Are you sure?" she asked gently.

I closed my eyes, letting the truth rise to the surface. "Yes," I whispered. "I can't stay here anymore."

A few days later, Nora arrived, clipboard in hand, her usual bright smile softened with understanding. As she walked through the house, I could tell she was choosing her words carefully, knowing this wasn't just a listing—it was a chapter of my life I was closing.

"It's a beautiful home, Lola," she said after walking through the rooms. "It won't take long to sell."

I nodded, holding back tears. "I just need to move on."

Putting the house on the market felt like another loss, another goodbye. But I reminded myself—I wasn't just leaving a house. I was making space for whatever God had next.

In the weeks that followed, I packed slowly, sorting through Derrick's things, deciding what to keep, what to donate, and what to release. Every item told a story. Every photograph held a moment suspended in time. Some days, I broke down, overwhelmed by grief. On other days, I smiled, remembering the love we shared.

One evening, as I boxed up some of Derrick's books, Mikaela sat beside me and placed her hand on mine.

"Mom," she said softly, "you don't have to rush this."

I met her gaze, my heart full of gratitude for the daughter who had been my rock through it all.

"I know," I whispered. "But I think I'm ready."

As difficult as it was, I knew I couldn't hold on to everything. I wanted Derrick's legacy to live on in the people who loved him, not just in the things he left behind. So I reached out to his brother and a few of his closest friends, inviting them over to go through his belongings and take anything that held special meaning.

When they arrived, there was an unspoken heaviness in the air—a quiet understanding that this moment was as much about grief as it was about love. We gathered in the living room, surrounded by Derrick's favorite books, his collection of watches, and the jackets he wore so often that they still carried his scent.

His brother, Marcus, picked up a leather-bound journal and smiled wistfully.

"He used to write everything down," he said, flipping through the pages. "Thoughts, ideas, random quotes. I'd love to keep this."

I nodded, a bittersweet warmth settling in my chest. "He'd want you to have it."

One by one, they chose items that connected them to Derrick—a framed photo from a fishing trip, his favorite Ravens hoodie, a book he'd once recommended. It wasn't about possessions; it was about holding onto pieces of him in ways that mattered.

At first, it was quiet, each of us lost in our own memories. Then someone chuckled, "Remember when Derrick tried to grill for the first time and nearly set the deck on fire?"

Laughter rippled through the room—tentative at first, then full and unrestrained.

It felt like Derrick was still there, in the stories, in the warmth that filled the spaces where sorrow had once suffocated. The night stretched on with more shared memories—his goofy impressions, his infamous dance moves, the way he always had the perfect comeback.

And in those moments, I felt something I hadn't in a long time.

Love.

Love for Derrick. Love for the people who had gathered to remember him. Love for the memories that grief could never erase.

By the end of the night, I realized that letting go didn't mean forgetting. It meant making space—for healing, for connection, for the kind of love that lingers far beyond a person's time on earth.

Derrick would always be a part of me, a part of all of us.

And in that moment, I knew I was taking another step toward healing.

The days that followed felt different—lighter yet still tinged with the ever-present ache of missing him. But something had shifted. The house no longer felt like a shrine to what I had lost but rather a space where love had once lived—and, in many ways, still did.

I found myself drawn to Derrick's journal, the one Marcus had taken. I had dozens of my own journals tucked away in drawers, but knowing Derrick had done the same—writing down his thoughts, ideas, and hopes—made me feel closer to him. The next day, I called Marcus and asked if I could see more of what Derrick had written.

When we met, he handed me the journal, a small smile tugging at his lips. "He had a lot to say," he said. "I think he was always writing to understand the world—and himself."

I ran my fingers over the worn cover before carefully opening it. The first page held a single quote, scribbled in Derrick's unmistakable handwriting:

"What we once enjoyed and deeply loved, we can never lose, for all that we love deeply becomes a part of us." – Helen Keller

Tears welled in my eyes as I read it again and again. Derrick had always been intentional—with how he lived, how he loved. He was the kind of man who left pieces of himself behind in ways that couldn't be boxed up or given away. His words, his presence, his impact—they were still here.

I flipped through the pages—some filled with reflections, others with quick notes and scattered ideas. There were lists of books he wanted to read, places he hoped to visit, and even a half-written letter addressed to me.

"If you're ever reading this, it means life happened in ways we didn't expect. And if you're hurting, I need you to know something: You are stronger than you think. You always have been. You don't need me to tell you that, but just in case you ever forget, let this be your reminder. Keep going. Keep living. Love big. Laugh hard. And when you're ready... let yourself be happy again."

I pressed the journal to my chest, letting the weight of his words settle into the deepest parts of me. I didn't know when I'd be ready to fully step into whatever came next—but I knew one thing for sure: Derrick would want me to.

And maybe, just maybe, I was finally ready to try.

Chapter 14

FINDING LIGHT IN NEW BEGINNINGS

> *"Every ending carries the quiet promise of a new beginning—if you're willing to embrace it."*

Within two months, the house was sold. The finality of it hit me as I handed over the keys, standing in the driveway one last time. I whispered a silent prayer, thanking God for the love Derrick and I shared, the memories we built, and the strength to move forward.

With the sale behind me, I focused on finding a new home—one that was just for me. Not the home Derrick and I had planned for, but the one I would create on my own.

The search wasn't easy. Every house I toured stirred a wave of emotions—Would Derrick have liked this place? The layout? The neighborhood? But deep down, I knew this wasn't about our past. It was about my future.

After weeks of looking, I found it. A beautiful, modern condo in the heart of the city, overlooking the skyline. It was smaller, quieter, and just enough for me. As I stepped inside for the first time as the owner, I felt something unexpected.

Peace.

It was a fresh start, a blank canvas where I could redefine what home meant to me. I took my time decorating—choosing colors that brought warmth, art that inspired me, and furniture that made the space feel like mine.

One evening, curled up on my new couch with a glass of wine, watching the city lights flicker in the distance, I realized something.

This wasn't the life I had planned. But it was the life I was choosing to embrace.

And with that, I took my first deep breath in what felt like forever. I was ready for whatever came next.

Still, even with a new home and a growing sense of peace, uneasiness lingered. The questions haunted me—Why did this happen? Why now? Why us?

I knew I couldn't carry the weight alone. I needed help sorting through the grief, the rage, the sadness, the confusion that still came in relentless waves.

People often shy away from therapy, fearing judgment or believing they should be strong enough to handle things on their own. But I knew better. I had God. I had prayer. I had the unwavering support of my friends and family. But I also needed professional guidance—someone to help me navigate emotions too heavy to carry by myself.

So, I made the call.

Sitting in the therapist's office for the first time, I felt exposed, raw, and uncertain. But as I spoke—unraveling the pain I had buried deep inside—something shifted. I wasn't just surviving; I was beginning to heal.

Therapy became my safe space, a place where I could release emotions I had been too afraid to admit, even to myself. Each session helped me process the weight of my loss, the love I had for Derrick, and the life I was now learning to rebuild.

One evening, after a particularly emotional session, I sat in my car staring at the sky. The stars twinkled above me, and for the first time in a long while, I allowed myself to simply breathe.

I wasn't okay yet—but I was getting there. Healing wasn't a straight path; it was a journey. And I was finally ready to take the next step.

It had been about three months since Derrick passed, and summer had arrived in full force. Therapy was going well, and for the first time in a while, I was starting to feel a little more like myself. The grief was still there, but it no longer consumed me.

One evening, as I sat with my friends, Latonya brought up something I had nearly forgotten.

"Lola, we already paid for those trips. And girl, we are still going," she said, her voice leaving no room for debate. I hesitated for a moment, but deep down, I knew she was right. Derrick wouldn't have wanted me to put my life on hold. "What's first?" Latonya asked, her eyes full of excitement. I took a deep breath and smiled. "First stop, Puerto Rico."

The thought of getting away—feeling the sun on my skin and simply existing without the weight of grief—felt like something I desperately needed. This trip wouldn't erase the pain, but maybe, just maybe, it would remind me that joy was still possible. And for the first time in a long time, I was ready to embrace it.

Puerto Rico was everything I didn't know I needed. The moment we landed, the warm breeze wrapped around me like a comforting embrace. It felt different—lighter, freer. For the first time in months, I wasn't waking up with the same heavy sadness pressing against my chest. My friends had one mission: to remind me how to live again.

We spent our days soaking up the sun on pristine beaches, letting the waves wash over our feet as we laughed and reminisced. Latonya, always the adventurer, convinced us to hike through El Yunque. Standing beneath a cascading waterfall, I closed my eyes and let the cool water rush over me. It felt like a renewal—a moment of clarity, a reminder that I was still here, still standing.

Our nights were filled with music and dancing in Old San Juan. One evening, Shelly pulled me onto the dance floor, insisting, "Lola, tonight, you're not a widow. You're just a woman having fun." And for the first time in a long while, I let go. I moved with the music, laughed freely, and simply existed.

One night, as we sat by the beach watching waves under the moonlight, Karen reached over and squeezed my hand. "You know Derrick would love seeing you like this, right?"

I nodded, swallowing the lump in my throat. "I know," I whispered. And for the first time, saying it didn't hurt as much.

This trip wasn't about escaping grief—it was about learning to live alongside it. It was about remembering that even in loss, life still held beauty, adventure, and joy.

As our trip came to an end, I realized something: I wasn't just surviving anymore. I was starting to live again.

Returning home from Puerto Rico, I felt different—lighter, more open to what was next. Grief still lived within me, but it no longer consumed me. Therapy was helping. My friends were my lifeline. And I was beginning to see a future that wasn't just about surviving but truly living.

A few weeks later, I found myself packing again—this time for Greece. Our long-awaited trip, once planned with Derrick in mind, had become a journey of sisterhood, healing, and rediscovery.

The moment we arrived in Santorini, I was in awe. The whitewashed buildings, the deep blue sea, the golden sunset stretching across the horizon—it was breathtaking. We spent our days exploring ancient ruins, savoring fresh seafood, and soaking in the beauty of a place that felt almost too magical to be real.

One evening, as we sipped wine on our villa's balcony, Latonya looked at me and said, "Lola, you're glowing." I smiled—a real, genuine smile. "I think I'm finally starting to feel like myself again."

But the truth was, I wasn't the same woman I had been before. Grief had changed me. But so had love. So had friendship. So had this journey of learning to embrace life again, even after loss.

Standing on the cliffs of Oie, watching the sun dip below the horizon, I closed my eyes and whispered a quiet prayer. "Thank you, God, for bringing me through."

When I opened my eyes, I knew I was ready for whatever came next. I embraced life—fully, unapologetically, with a heart open to new possibilities. I threw myself into work: teaching, planning conferences, and traveling. My days were full, my calendar packed, and for the first time in a long while, I felt like I was moving forward.

Summer became a season of healing and rediscovery. Trips, concerts, cookouts, comedy shows—event after event, distraction after distraction. But it wasn't just about staying busy; it was about reclaiming joy. Laughter wasn't forced. Moments weren't overshadowed by grief. Memories were created without guilt.

Puerto Rico was just the beginning. Greece was unforgettable. Then came spontaneous road trips, beach weekends, and rooftop brunches with my girls. Each experience reminded me that I was still here, still living, still capable of happiness.

One evening, after a long day of teaching, I sat in my new condo, sipping a glass of wine and reflecting on how far I had come. My home was finally beginning to feel like mine—not just a place I had moved to, but a space I had made my own. The walls were filled with photos of Mikaela, my friends, and moments that made me smile.

I exhaled deeply, realizing that while grief was still present, it no longer held me hostage. I had survived. I had grown. And most importantly, I had given myself permission to live again.

As I turned out the lights and climbed into bed, I whispered the same words that had carried me through the darkest days: "Thank you, God, for bringing me through."

Stepping into a new season, I found myself settling into a rhythm no longer defined by grief but by purpose, growth, and gratitude. Therapy remained a safe space—one where I could process emotions without judgment. I no longer felt burdened by the "why" of Derrick's passing. I was learning to accept that some questions would never have answers—and that was okay.

The Color of Pretty movement was thriving. The mentorship program was expanding, and I was being invited to speak at more conferences and events than ever before. Each time I took the stage, I shared my story—not just of success but of loss, resilience, and rebuilding. Women approached me afterward with tears in their eyes, thanking me for giving voice to what they had felt but couldn't express.

One evening, after wrapping up a panel discussion in Chicago, I received a text from Mikaela: *Mom, I'm so proud of you. You are really walking in your purpose.* Tears welled in my eyes as I read her message. She had been my motivation through everything, and now she was seeing me—not just as her mother but as a woman standing in her own power.

That night, I sat in my hotel room, staring out at the city lights. I thought about everything I had lost, but more importantly, everything I had gained: peace, purpose, and a deeper appreciation for life.

I knew there would still be hard days—moments when grief would creep in unexpectedly—but I also knew I had the tools, the support, and the faith to keep moving forward.

For the first time in a long time, I wasn't just surviving.

As summer faded into autumn and the days grew shorter, I felt a shift within me. The excitement of traveling, working, and staying busy had kept my mind occupied, but now, in the quiet, something else was settling in—an overwhelming sense of sadness.

Even though therapy was going well, I could feel depression beginning to take hold, a heavy weight pressing on my chest. I didn't understand it. Hadn't I been doing everything right? I was working, thriving in my purpose, surrounded by love and support. Still, something felt like it was slipping—my confidence, my energy, my sense of peace.

I brought it up in my next therapy session, hoping for answers, maybe even a solution. Instead, my therapist nodded gently. "Grief has its peaks and valleys," she said. "Now that the holidays are approaching and the days are getting darker sooner, your mood may be shifting. That's normal."

Normal.

But it didn't feel normal. It felt like I was unraveling again, like the very tools I had offered other women—hope, strength, resilience—weren't working for me.

"How do I get out of this?" I asked, my voice barely above a whisper.

"There's no 'getting out' of grief," she said. "But you can move through it. That means acknowledging the hard moments, making space for them, and giving yourself grace. You don't have to fight it alone."

Her words stayed with me long after the session ended. Maybe that was the problem—I had been trying to fight it. Trying to outwork my grief, to keep myself so busy I wouldn't have to feel it. But it was still there, waiting for me in the quiet.

That night, I sat in my living room with a cup of tea wrapped in the comfort of my favorite blanket. I let myself feel it all—the sadness, the loneliness, the longing. And then, just as my therapist had said, I gave myself grace.

I didn't have to have it all figured out.

I just had to keep moving.

As the days grew colder and the holiday season approached, I leaned into the small things that brought me comfort—morning journaling, long walks, warm baths, exercise, and intentional moments of stillness. Therapy continued to help, even on the days I resisted it. Some days were easier than others, but I was learning that healing wasn't linear.

One afternoon, while organizing old conference notes, I came across a journal entry I'd written years ago when I first started The Color of Pretty. It was filled with affirmations, goals, and reminders of why I began.

You are worthy of joy, even in your hardest seasons.

Tears welled in my eyes as I read my own words. I had poured so much of myself into uplifting others, but in that moment, I realized I needed to pour back into me.

So, I started doing just that.

I reconnected with friends—not for distraction, but for real, honest conversations. I let myself cry when I needed to, but I also made room for laughter. I made plans for the holidays instead of dreading them, ensuring I wouldn't be sitting alone in silence.

Then, one evening, I received a message from a woman who had attended my last conference:

Lola, I just wanted to say thank you. Your words changed my life. I'm going through a tough time, but because of what you taught me, I know I'll get through it. You reminded me that even in my darkest moments, I am still enough.

I stared at the message, my heart swelling.

That was it. That was my answer.

Even in my own grief, my purpose remained. Even in my uncertainty, I was still making an impact.

I wiped away my tears, whispered a prayer of gratitude, and reminded myself—just as I had reminded so many other women before—that I was still worthy. Still strong. Still enough.

And I would keep going.

STEPPING INTO THE NEW YEAR

As the holidays passed and the new year approached, I felt a shift—not a complete transformation, but a small, steady spark of renewal. I had made it through one of the hardest seasons of my life, and though grief still lingered in unexpected moments, I was learning to carry it with grace.

Instead of writing a list of resolutions, I chose one word to define my year: ***Reclaim.***

Reclaim my joy. Reclaim my confidence. Reclaim my purpose.

I sat down with my team to map out the next steps for The Color of Pretty. The conference was expanding, and with more women reaching out for mentorship, I knew it was time to take things to the next level.

"What if we take the conference on tour?" I suggested during our first meeting of the year.

The room buzzed with excitement. We had done the work locally—now it was time to reach women in cities across the country, maybe even internationally.

"We can call it The Pretty Power Tour," Latonya said, grinning.

I smiled, feeling a sense of purpose reignite within me. This was what I was meant to do: help women rediscover themselves, just as I was rediscovering me.

SAYING YES TO ME

While I poured into my work, I also made a promise to myself: this year, I would say yes to experiences that poured into me.

I booked a solo trip to Paris—a dream I had put off for years. I signed up for a dance class just for fun. I allowed myself to be open to love again—not rushing, not searching, just open to the idea that joy could find me in unexpected places.

One evening, as I stood on my balcony overlooking the city, I felt something I hadn't felt in a long time.

Not just peace.

Hope.

I had survived the unimaginable. But more than that, I was learning to live again.

And for the first time in a long time, I knew this was only the beginning.

It had been almost a year since Derrick passed, and the start of a new year felt like the fresh beginning I desperately needed. The Color of Pretty Conference Tour was officially set to kick off in September, my vacation plans were lined up, Mikaela was thriving in her own life, and for the first time in a while, I was starting to truly breathe again.

I could feel myself relaxing, settling into a new rhythm—one that no longer revolved around grief but focused on rebuilding. My confidence was returning, little by little. I was rediscovering parts of myself that had been buried under pain, and with each passing day, I felt stronger.

And then, a thought crept in—one I never imagined entertaining so soon.

DATING.

Not in a rushed, desperate way, but in a *maybe I could open my heart again* kind of way.

It wasn't about replacing Derrick or filling a void. It was about allowing myself to believe that love, companionship, and even simple joy were still possible for me.

One evening, over dinner with my girlfriends, Latonya brought it up first.

"So… have you thought about dating again?" she asked, raising an eyebrow over her glass of wine.

I sighed, then smiled. "I mean, kind of. I'm not actively looking, but I'm also not completely shutting it out."

Karen grinned. "That's progress."

Shelly, ever the romantic, clapped her hands together. "I love this for you! Just be open, that's all."

I nodded, sipping my drink. *Be open.*

For so long, my life had been about survival. But now? Now, I wanted to thrive.

And maybe—just maybe—that meant making room for something new.

A HEART OPEN TO POSSIBILITY

As the weeks passed, I focused on my work, my friendships, and my personal growth. But in the quiet moments—between conference planning and late-night journaling—the thought of dating lingered.

One evening, Mikaela and I were catching up over dinner when she casually dropped a bombshell.

"So… when are you going to put yourself out there again?" she asked, twirling her fork in her pasta.

I nearly choked on my drink. "Excuse me?"

She smirked. "Mom, you're an incredible woman. You have so much love to give, and I know Dad wouldn't want you to close yourself off forever."

I sighed, setting down my fork. "It's not that simple, Mikaela."

"I know," she said softly. "But I just want you to be happy."

Her words stayed with me long after dinner ended.

The truth was, I *was* happy—not in the way I once imagined, but in a way that felt real. I had rebuilt my life, found my strength, and rediscovered joy in the things I loved. But was I ready to share that joy with someone else?

A few weeks later, Latonya convinced me to join her at a networking event.

"It's not a dating event," she promised. "But if you happen to meet someone interesting, it wouldn't hurt."

Dressed in a sleek, confidence-boosting outfit, I walked into the venue with an open mind. The night was full of great conversations and connections, but one encounter stood out.

His name was James—an entrepreneur with a passion for philanthropy. He wasn't overly charming or pushy, just genuine and easy to talk to.

By the end of the evening, he handed me his card. "I'd love to grab coffee sometime—no pressure, just good conversation."

For the first time in a long time, I didn't panic. I didn't feel guilty. I just felt... curious.

That night, as I lay in bed, I stared at the card on my nightstand.

Maybe it was time to take a step forward—not just in life, but in love.

And maybe, just maybe, I was ready.

I had learned to embrace my journey—every high, every low, every unexpected turn.

The grief still existed, but it no longer consumed me. Instead, it lived alongside the love I would always have for Derrick—a reminder of a chapter that shaped me but did not define me.

Chapter 15

EMBRACING THE PRESENT

"True joy comes from within—from embracing life fully, from showing up for yourself, from choosing to believe that you are worthy of all the good things still to come."

As I stood on stage at the Color of Pretty conference, looking out at the sea of women—each on her own journey of healing, growth, and self-discovery—I felt an overwhelming sense of gratitude. This moment was bigger than me. Bigger than the pain I had endured, the setbacks I had faced, or the love I had lost. It was the result of every step I had taken to rebuild myself, to rise from the ashes of my past, and to create something meaningful—not just for me, but for others.

I gripped the microphone, my heart pounding—not with fear, but with a profound sense of purpose. The women before me weren't just an audience; they were reflections of the many versions of myself I had been—the broken, the lost, the resilient, the reborn. Their eyes held stories of their own—some filled with sorrow, others brimming with hope. In that moment, I knew I had come full circle.

The words flowed effortlessly, not from a script but from the depths of my soul.

"We are more than what we have lost. We are more than the love that left us, the dreams that crumbled, and the pain that threatened to define us. We are more than the doubts that whispered we weren't enough. Because look at us now. Standing. Thriving. Rising."

Applause rippled through the room, but what moved me most were the nods, the tear-filled eyes, the silent acknowledgments of women who understood—who felt seen, who knew, perhaps for the first time, that they weren't alone.

When the conference ended, I lingered, letting the moment sink in. The woman who once questioned her worth, who once wondered if she would ever feel whole again, had become a beacon of hope for others.

As I stepped into the cool evening air, Mikaela was waiting for me. My daughter. My heart. My greatest reminder that love, even when tested, is never truly lost. She had grown into a force of her own, stepping into her purpose with grace and confidence.

"Mom," she said, wrapping her arms around me, "you were incredible."

I smiled, holding her tightly, remembering all the moments I had doubted myself—all the times I'd questioned whether I was doing enough, being enough. But looking at her now, I knew: I had done something right.

We walked together to the restaurant, the city lights casting a golden glow on the streets. Over dinner, she spoke of her dreams, her next steps, and the life she was creating for herself. As I listened, I realized healing isn't just about letting go of the past—

it's about stepping fully into the present and embracing the future with open arms.

"Mom," she said, raising her glass, "to new beginnings."

I lifted mine, a smile tugging at my lips. "To love, to resilience, and to never giving up on yourself."

The glasses clinked, a quiet but powerful affirmation of everything we had overcome.

As the conversation deepened, Mikaela looked at me thoughtfully. "Do you think everything you went through was necessary?"

I exhaled, considering her question. "Necessary? I don't know if I'd call it that. But I do know it shaped me. Every heartbreak, every disappointment, every time I felt lost—it all led me here. And I wouldn't change that."

She nodded, taking it in. "So, you don't regret anything?"

I laughed softly. "Oh, I regret plenty. But I don't let those regrets define me anymore. I used to believe my mistakes made me unworthy of love, of success, of happiness. But I've learned that mistakes don't make us unworthy—they make us human. And growth comes from what we choose to do next."

Mikaela reached across the table, squeezing my hand. "I'm proud of you."

Tears welled in my eyes, but this time, they weren't from pain. They came from the sheer beauty of the moment—of being seen, of being understood.

As the night went on, I found myself reflecting on the women who had shaped my journey. The friends who had held me up when I was at my lowest, the mentors who had guided me, even the relationships that had ended painfully—each had played a role in my transformation.

I thought about the love I had lost and the love I had found—not just in others, but in myself. I had spent so much of my life searching for validation, believing that love from someone else would complete me. But now, sitting here, I knew the truth: I was already whole.

"What's next for you?" Mikaela asked.

I smiled. "More. More healing, more growth, more impact. I want to keep building this movement—to help women see their worth, to remind them that no matter what they've been through, they can rise."

She nodded. "You've turned your pain into something powerful, Mom. And that's why you're unstoppable."

I looked around, taking in the warmth of the restaurant and the hum of life all around us. I had spent years believing happiness was fragile, something that could slip through my fingers at any moment. But now I understood that true joy comes from within—from embracing life fully, showing up for yourself, and choosing to believe you are worthy of all the good things still to come.

I was no longer just surviving.

I was truly living.

For the first time in a long time, I wasn't looking back with regret or ahead with fear. I was here, now, in this moment—whole, free, and ready for whatever came next.

The best wasn't just yet to come.

It was already happening.

And I was ready for it.

As we finished our meal and stepped outside, the city buzzed with life, the air humming with possibility. Mikaela looped her arm through mine, and we walked in comfortable silence. The past no longer held me captive. The future no longer filled me with doubt.

I had built something beautiful—not just the movement, but a life I was proud of. A life where I was seen, heard, and valued. A life where I knew, deep in my bones, that I was enough.

As we stood at the curb, the evening air still cool against my skin, a wave of contentment washed over me. The city lights flickered, casting a glow on everything they touched, and for the first time in a long time, I felt at peace. Mikaela's arm rested lightly through mine, her presence a steady reminder of the strength I had found in myself and in our bond.

Then, as if the world had paused for just a moment, I saw him—a man walking toward us with quiet confidence. His eyes locked with mine from across the street, and it was as though time stood still. He moved closer, his gaze unwavering, and I felt my heart skip a beat. As he neared, he smiled and said, in a voice both familiar and strange, "You're Lola, aren't you?"

I froze, unsure whether I had heard him correctly. My heart raced as I looked into his eyes, drawn by the deep, searching intensity behind them. There was something about him—something that stirred memories and emotions I couldn't quite place.

"Yes," I replied softly, my voice barely above a whisper. As the word left my lips, the smile that spread across his face felt like a promise, one that would change everything.

For a brief moment, the world around us seemed to fade, and all I could see was him. Then, just as suddenly as he had appeared, his presence filled the space between us, a new chapter unfolding before my eyes.

We both smiled, and with that smile, I knew something had shifted. Something was about to begin.

And with that, the night—my new beginning—took a turn I hadn't expected.

TO THE WIDOW WHO FEELS BROKEN

If you're reading this, my heart is with you. I know the weight of grief—the unbearable silence, the nights that feel endless. I know what it means to wake up reaching for someone who's no longer there, to replay the memories, to wonder how life moves forward when part of your heart is gone.

But dear widow, you are not alone.

Your love was real. Your loss is real. And so is the pain that lingers in the spaces where love once lived. Even in the depths of sorrow, I want you to know that you are still here for a reason. God is not finished with your story.

Grief will come in waves—some gentle, some fierce. Some days, you'll stand strong; other days, you'll crumble. Both are okay. Healing isn't about forgetting but about learning to carry love and loss together.

You may feel shattered, but even broken pieces can be remade into something beautiful. Your life still holds purpose. Your joy, though different now, will return. You'll learn to love the memories without being trapped in them. You will smile again—not because you've moved on, but because you've moved forward with love still in your heart.

So when the nights feel heavy, when loneliness threatens to consume you, remember this: God is near to the brokenhearted (Psalm 34:18). He sees your tears. He hears your prayers. And He walks with you, even when you can't see the path ahead.

You are not just a widow. You are a woman of strength. A woman of love. A woman whose story is still unfolding.

Take your time. Breathe. And when you're ready, step forward—one piece at a time.

PRACTICAL GUIDANCE FOR NAVIGATING GRIEF

1. Allow Yourself to Grieve

- There is no timeline for grief. Feel your emotions without guilt.

- Journaling your thoughts and emotions can help you process your pain.

2. Find a Support System

- Surround yourself with people who understand—whether it's family, friends, a grief support group, or a faith community.

- Consider therapy or counseling to navigate complex emotions.

3. Honor Their Memory in Your Own Way

- Keep a memory box with letters, photos, or special items.

- Start a tradition in their honor—lighting a candle, writing them letters, or celebrating their birthday in a way that brings comfort.

4. Take Small Steps Forward

- Start by setting small goals—even simple things like going for a walk, reading a book, or engaging in a hobby.

- Be patient with yourself. Healing isn't linear, and there will be hard days.

5. Reconnect with Yourself & Your Purpose

- Rediscover who you are outside of being a wife. What passions or dreams have you put on hold?

- Consider getting involved in volunteering, creative expression, or helping others in their grief journey.

A PRAYER FOR WIDOWS

Heavenly Father,

I come to You with a heart that aches—empty and longing for comfort. I don't always understand why loss comes, but I know You are close to the brokenhearted. Wrap me in Your peace when the loneliness feels overwhelming. Give me the strength to rise each day and keep going, even when it feels impossible.

Help me carry both love and grief, knowing that loss does not erase the beauty of what I shared. Guide me through this season of healing, remind me of my purpose, and help me find joy again—not because I've forgotten, but because I'm learning to live fully in the love You've given me.

Amen.

AFFIRMATIONS FOR HEALING & STRENGTH

💜 I am allowed to grieve at my own pace.

💜 My pain does not define me—my strength does.

💜 Love does not end with loss; it lives on in my heart.

💜 I am not alone—God walks with me in my sorrow.

💜 Joy will return to me in its own time.

💜 My life still has purpose, and I am open to discovering it.

CLOSING WORDS

Wherever you are in your grief journey, know that you are not alone. There is no "right" way to heal and no shame in taking your time. Give yourself permission to feel, to cry, to rest, and to rebuild at your own pace. You are strong, even on the days you feel weak. You are loved, even when loneliness tells you otherwise. And you are still here for a reason—one that will reveal itself in time.

May you find peace, purpose, and renewed strength as you walk this path—one step at a time.

With love and understanding,

DISCUSSION QUESTIONS

The following questions are designed to help you reflect on your personal journey as you read *Pretty in Pieces*. This book explores themes of self-worth, healing, love, loss, resilience, and empowerment, all of which may resonate with different aspects of your life.

Use these questions to:

- Look inward and examine how your experiences align with the themes in the book.

- Identify areas for personal growth and healing as you navigate your own challenges.

- Spark deep conversations with yourself, a trusted friend, or a book club.

There are no right or wrong answers—only an opportunity to learn, heal, and grow. Take your time as you reflect, and allow yourself to be honest and open about where you are in your journey.

SELF-WORTH & PERSONAL GROWTH

1. Have you ever struggled with feeling "not enough" in any area of your life? Where do you think those beliefs came from, and how have they shaped your choices?

2. Lola learns to embrace self-love and confidence over time. What are some ways you can affirm your own worth, regardless of external validation?

3. Think about a time when you had to redefine yourself after a major life event. How did that experience change you?

HEALING & LETTING GO

1. What past pain, heartbreak, or loss are you still carrying? How can you begin to release it and move forward?

2. Have you ever held onto a relationship (romantic or otherwise) that no longer served you? What made you stay, and what ultimately helped you let go?

3. Grief and loss can be life-altering. How do you process grief, and what helps you find peace in difficult moments?

RELATIONSHIPS & BOUNDARIES

1. Think about your past or present relationships. Have you ever settled for less than you deserved? What lessons did you take from those experiences?

2. Lola's friendships played a key role in her growth. Who are the people in your life that truly uplift and support you? How can you strengthen those connections?

3. What boundaries do you need to set (or reinforce) in your personal or professional relationships to protect your peace?

PURPOSE & EMPOWERMENT

1. Lola turned her pain into purpose by creating *The Color of Pretty*. What challenges have you faced that could be transformed into something meaningful for yourself or others?

2. If you fully embraced your confidence and stepped into your power, what dreams or goals would you pursue without hesitation?

3. How do you define success and fulfillment in your life today? Has that definition changed over time?

REFLECTION & MOVING FORWARD

1. What was the most eye-opening or emotional moment for you while reading this book? Why did it stand out?

2. If you could go back and give advice to your younger self, what would you say?

3. What is one commitment you can make today to prioritize your healing, growth, or self-worth moving forward?

FINAL THOUGHTS

These questions are meant to guide you toward greater self-awareness, healing, and empowerment. You don't have to answer them all at once—take your time, revisit them as needed, and allow yourself to sit with whatever emotions arise. Remember, your journey is yours alone, and every step forward is a victory.

You are enough.
You are worthy.
And your story is still unfolding.

ACKNOWLEDGEMENT

Jeremiah 29:11
"For I know the plans I have for you," declares the Lord, "plans to prosper you and not to harm you, plans to give you hope and a future."

The inspiration for this book came from my own journey of healing. As I walked through my pain, God placed it on my heart to share my truth: the good, the bad, and the ugly. This book is more than just my story; it is a testament to resilience, faith, and the power of transformation.

I believe that healing comes through honesty, and by laying bare my experiences, I hope to create a space for others to find their own strength. This book is not just for me; it is for every person who has ever felt broken, lost, or uncertain about how to move forward. I pray that these words bring comfort, encouragement, and the reminder that healing is possible no matter how dark things may seem.

May this book not only help me heal but also touch the lives of people around the world, reminding them that their pain does not define them but rather refines them.

God, I thank you!!!!

In addition, I want to express my heartfelt gratitude to my mother, Valerie Miller, whose love and strength have been a guiding light in my life. To my daughter, Dashaira Bennett, you are my greatest blessing and inspiration to keep pushing forward.

I also want to thank my family for their support, along with some of the most amazing friends a woman could ever ask for. Your unwavering support, love, and encouragement have carried me through some of my darkest moments.

A special mention goes to these incredible women—Tonya McCleary, Adriane Jackson, Kim Swann-Ndiaye, Nicole Webb, Kelly Dickens, Linda Stewart and Samantha Ellis. You have each played a unique and irreplaceable role in my journey. Your presence, wisdom, and sisterhood have lifted me up when I needed it most.

And to my **Sisterfriend group,** words cannot fully express how much you mean to me. You are my tribe, safe space, and reminder that true friendship is a bond that cannot be broken.

Thank you all for standing by me, believing in me, and loving me unconditionally. This journey would not have been the same without you.

To the Rhoney family, I want to express my deepest gratitude. From the very beginning, you welcomed me with open arms, embracing me. Your love, kindness, and unwavering support have meant more to me than words can ever convey.

Eric Rhoney, thank you. Thank you for loving me in a way that made me feel safe, for protecting me when I needed it most, and for always taking care of me in big and small ways. The memories we shared, the laughter that filled our days, and even the lessons learned along the way will forever be etched in my heart.

Though you are no longer here physically, I carry you with me always. I find peace in knowing that you are resting with God, free from struggle and pain. Your spirit lives on in the love you gave, the impact you made, and the legacy you left behind. I will cherish every moment we had together, holding onto them as a reminder that love never truly fades; it simply transforms. Thank you for everything, Eric. You will always be a part of me. Rest well, HUSBAND!!!!

Finally, I want to take a moment to thank **ME**. Girl, you did it! You pushed through when it was hard, when it felt impossible, when the weight of it all seemed too much to bear. It was tough, it was challenging, and it was emotional. There were days you felt stuck, days when frustration, sadness, and confusion tried to hold you back. But you kept going. You refused to give up. You showed up for yourself time and time again.

This journey wasn't just about writing a book but healing, growing, and stepping fully into your power. And look at you now. You **did it**.

So, as you close this chapter and step into the next, remember the same words you have poured into others: **Be Bold. Be Brave. Be YOU.** Because confidence? **It looks damn good on YOU!** Keep shining, keep believing, and keep walking in your purpose.

ABOUT THE AUTHOR

Michelle E. Rhoney –

Hailing from the Charm City of Baltimore, MD, Michelle E. Rhoney has always been a natural-born leader. Her childhood was filled with adventure, resilience, and moments of deep reflection, shaping the woman she would become. Despite facing complicated memories and loneliness, she persevered, earning a B.S. in Business and Healthcare Administration from Sojourner Douglass College. She later obtained dual master's degrees in Human Resource Management and Public Administration from Towson University.

With 27+ years of experience in human resources, Michelle has established herself as a leader in her industry, providing innovative solutions in higher education, government, and healthcare. She is also an associate professor, teaching human resource courses at multiple higher education institutions. In addition to her corporate career, Michelle founded HR Innovations 3000, a consulting firm dedicated to strategic HR solutions and professional development.

Beyond her corporate achievements, Michelle is the author of *The Color of Pretty*, which has evolved into a foundation and a powerful movement dedicated to mentorship, self-love, and empowerment. The foundation has collaborated with mental health professionals, offering resources that support emotional well-being and confidence-building for women and young girls.

She has spearheaded transformative initiatives, including the annual Confidence Looks Good on You conference, designed to empower women of all ages. This dynamic event fosters self-assurance, personal growth, and resilience, equipping attendees with the tools and inspiration to embrace their worth and potential. Through engaging workshops, motivational speakers, and interactive sessions, the conference creates a supportive community where women can connect, learn, and thrive.

The *Confidence Looks Good on You* conference goes beyond motivation—it provides actionable strategies for women to step into their power in every aspect of life. Attendees gain insights on topics such as self-love, overcoming adversity, professional development, and personal branding. With a lineup of influential speakers, panel discussions, and hands-on activities, the event cultivates an atmosphere of encouragement and transformation.

In addition to the conference, she has introduced mentorship programs and networking opportunities that extend the impact beyond the event itself. Through these initiatives, women of all backgrounds can access the guidance, support, and resources needed to build confidence, pursue their dreams, and redefine success on their own terms.

With the release of her second book, The Color of Pieces, Michelle continues her mission of storytelling, healing, and transformation. This autobiographical, fictional memoir is deeply inspired by her real-life journey, offering readers an intimate look into love, loss, resilience, and self-discovery.

Michelle remains committed to mentorship, advocacy, and helping others embrace their worth. She currently resides in Maryland, enjoying life as an empty nester, and continues to uplift and inspire women through her writing, foundation, and advocacy work.

Confidence Looks on You!!

Be Bold,
Be Brave,
but most importantly

BE YOU!!!!

In life, there will be may times when your confidence is shaken,
non-existent, but what will you do?

CONTINUE THE JOURNEY WITH MICHELLE'S POWERFUL DEBUT: "THE COLOR OF PRETTY"

Before there was healing, there was hurt.
And before there was self-love, there was self-doubt.

If you've been moved by the message in this book, you'll want to dive deeper into Michelle Rhoney's powerful debut novel, *The Color of Pretty*—a fictionalized memoir that courageously confronts the realities of colorism, self-esteem, bullying, and emotional abandonment.

Told through the eyes of Lola, a dark-skinned Black woman navigating life's many challenges—from an absentee father to relentless teasing and internalized shame—*The Color of Pretty* is a deeply honest portrayal of how colorism can fracture identity and steal confidence. But through reflection, resilience, and radical self-love, Lola begins her journey toward healing and wholeness.

More than just a novel, *The Color of Pretty* is a movement that encourages women to do the work, seek help, and unearth the root of their pain—proving that confidence is not something you're born with, but something you build through courageous action.

Grab your copy today at
www.thecolorofpretty.com/shop
or search *The Color of Pretty* by
Michelle Williams on Amazon.

Because every shade of you is worthy. And
every story deserves to be seen.